FALLING FOR MY ENEMY

NATASHA L. BLACK

COPYRIGHT

MAGGIE

If the rumors were true, I was about to get an archenemy. I wasn't a superhero or anything, and I'd never had a real enemy before, unless you counted the really cute, thin cheerleaders in high school.

But this... This was some shit actually getting real.

"Good luck tonight," I said wryly to Mrs. Cooper when she came to pick her son up from daycare. "Brennan would not take his nap again today."

"Oh. Did he do the thing where he freaks out like the blanket is a poisonous snake or something? He's doing that at home at bedtime like I'm trying to kill him or something instead of just getting him to sleep at a decent time."

"Pretty much. It was all hands on deck in the toddler room at naptime. I even pulled Kim from pre-K to try and help out. But he wouldn't calm down."

"Maybe he's feeling our stress at home, you know? Because it's all over the factory now, that corporate is sending somebody to shut us down," she said.

"I'm sure that's not going to happen," I said cheerfully

as I handed over her grouchy two-year-old and his elephant backpack.

When she left, I popped my head into pre-K and motioned for Kim to leave the aide in charge. "That's the third one this week to tell me they're shutting down the factory," I said.

"What would we do? That's our entire group. They're all factory kids, Maggie," she said. "If that place shuts down, so do we."

"I know. There's not another big industry in town. This area can't handle a plant shutdown. It would basically kill the town. And they may be sending some guy from the parent company to do the dirty work of announcing it."

"Some a-hole city slicker?" Kim asked.

"Yes. But if it's more than a rumor, we're not going without a fight. One man shouldn't have the kind of power to do that, to go ruin an entire way of life of so many for profit. It makes me mad."

"It makes me depressed. I'll have to go work at the hospital daycare in Pendleton or else go back to school," Kim said.

"You're a great early childhood teacher. They'd hire you at the school in a heartbeat."

"Yeah, at less than I make here. And teaching who? Families will move out of town for jobs," she said dismally.

"Okay, now that I've depressed you further, back to your happy place. I'll keep you posted," I said.

But I meant what I'd said. I wasn't going to let some rich, business suit-wearing creep shut down the factory that happened to be the lifeblood of the area.

By the time I got off work and left Helen in charge, I'd had four more factory employees confide their worry to me about a closing. When I got home, I called my mom. She was working the front desk at the family B&B.

"What have you heard about a corporate executive coming to shut down the plant?" I said.

"All I know is I've got a reservation here for a Jeremiah Leeds who's paying with a corporate-issued expense account card out of Boston. He'll be here for a week. It doesn't take a whole week to shut down a plant surely. Maybe it's just a quality inspection."

"I don't know," I said. "But I'm pretty sure everything this Jeremiah Leeds character stands for is going to be the opposite of what we need. But if he thinks we're just going to fold up and cry, he's underestimated us. I've spent too long building up this daycare business and making a success of it to go and let someone destroy it and most of the jobs in this town along with it."

"That's my girl," she said. "But remember, you'll catch more flies with honey than with vinegar. You have to kill them with kindness."

"What if you don't want to catch the flies, Mom? What if you just want to swat them?"

"All I know is you get better results being sweet and minding your manners. Maybe if this fellow likes you—"

"Do *not* tell me you're going to suggest I seduce a corporate drone sent to ruin all our lives," I warned.

"Well, maybe not him, but maybe he'll bring a friend."

"Do you think he's going to bring a friend along to shut down the plant? It's not a house party in Jane Austen, Mom. No one is bringing their handsome, eligible friends around for me to meet," I quipped.

"You're so funny. And single. Try using that brain of yours to get a man," she said.

"I'll keep that in mind," I said.

"Have you tried that Tinder thing I've been hearing about?" she asked.

"MOM!"

2

JEREMIAH

My plane landed at the nearest airport, twenty-five miles from my destination. I rented a car and followed the GPS to my lodgings. The place was too small to have any chain hotels—definitely not Four Seasons material. So I was staying at some locally owned inn that was likely to be some crappy AirBnB over someone's garage. I braced myself for a few nights of roughing it. I was really going to owe myself a vacation after this stop.

It wasn't exactly my idea of a fun assignment—go inspect a low-performing plant and shut it down so we can outsource fabrication and packaging overseas. It would save a fortune in production costs, but it was a miserable job taking away people's livelihood. It wasn't what I set out to do in my career.

I pulled in to a parking lot before an old Victorian-styled building complete with white gingerbread scrolls on the eaves and a fanlight over the door. The Beaumont Estate, the tasteful brass plaque read. I shouldered my bag and went inside. Maybe my accommodations wouldn't be as bad as I had feared.

The desk clerk was a knockout. A mane of fiery red hair waving over her shoulders, all curves and a sweet smile. She lifted her eyes from the book she was reading, marked her page with a slip of paper and looked at me. She gave me a dazzling smile that made my blood hum in my veins. God, she was gorgeous. My body lit up at her grin and I smiled back at her giving her my flirtatious best.

"Good evening," she said, "Welcome to the Beaumont. Is it your first time as our guest?" she asked. Her voice was lower than I expected and just as sexy as the rest of her.

"Yes, I'm afraid so. I'm new in town," I said.

"Well, I've lived here all my life. I know the best spots for bass fishing, and there's a hill south of town where the sunsets are incredible. If you want fine dining, your upscale restaurants are over in Pendleton, but we've got Cecil's Bar & Grill here in town. They do terrific steak dinners and the queso is... Well, if Meg Ryan had been eating that instead of a sandwich in When Harry Met Sally, she wouldn't have had to fake it, if you know what I mean."

Her sly smile was enough to undo me. She had just offered to take me bass fishing, which I wasn't remotely qualified to do, and alluded to an onscreen orgasm. This was my kind of woman.

"Then I should go try that queso. I've never had an orgasmic appetizer before. I feel like I'm missing out," I said.

"You should," she agreed. "And maybe I'll run into you there."

"I certainly wouldn't turn down a friendly face," I said.

"I'm Maggie Carson, owners' daughter. I run the daycare out by the factory, but I pitch in here sometimes. You need anything while you're staying with us, you just let me know."

"Nice to meet you, Maggie. I'm Jeremiah," I said.

I held out my hand for hers. She shook my hand, that gorgeous smile still in place. I wanted to kiss her. The thought caught me as much off guard as the touch of her hand, small and soft in mine. The sizzle ran up my arm like I'd been shocked. I fought the urge to pull her closer, to lean across the desk, put my hands in her hair and kiss the smile off her face.

This trip to the backwoods just started looking a lot better. I hadn't had a lover since my breakup with Lydia months ago. I didn't do casual sex or hookups, but a week with Maggie Carson felt like an exception. I never reacted this way, like a teenager, to some woman I'd only just met. The chemistry even in our handshake was palpable.

"Let me see here, what's your reservation under?" she said, tapping the screen of a tablet.

"My name is Jeremiah Leeds. It was booked under the Hadley Corporation," I told her.

Just like that, her smile slipped. When it returned, it was a dimmer, more formal version.

"Here on business then. You won't be needing a tour guide," she said, her voice cool. She had just rescinded the nine o'clock queso invitation when she heard my company name.

"Do you have some connection with Hadley?" I asked.

"Just that more than half the county relies on the factory for our livelihood. And you're here, if I'm not mistaken, to shut it down."

"I'm not at liberty to discuss my project," I said, my tone matching hers.

"You'll have to go on Amazon to order crime scene tape for when you're done. The lumberyard here doesn't sell 'police line do not cross'. And you're basically here to commit murder. Of my whole town. My mom had you booked on the second floor at the back, but I've moved you to the third floor, with a nice eastern view of the sunrise. Curtains would spoil that pretty view, so I hope you like waking up early," she said briskly and handed me a key.

"Do you have bell service? Elevator?"

"The elevator is only for disabled accessibility. You look able-bodied to me," she said.

"Thanks for noticing," I said, "Are we still on for queso?"

"Oh, I wish I could," she said with a saccharine smile, "but I just remembered I have an appointment."

"If you change your mind, you know where to find me," I said, "Third floor. Facing east," I smirked at her.

Up in my room, I went over my notes. I was going to conduct a thorough inspection before I made my recommendation. Part of me held out hope that I could suggest keeping the plant open. The girl downstairs was cute—strangely blunt and forceful about the factory closing—but cute. I wasn't ruling her out as an option. If she thought there were hidden depths to sleepy little towns, I could show her there was more charm to a city boy than met the eye.

I called my brother Tyler to let him know I made it in okay.

"How's the room? Is it some old woman's creepy basement?" he asked.

"No, it's not very big, but it's nice. It's an old house remodeled as a B&B. This place could attract tourists if it was marketed right. It's quaint, pretty streets and that kind of thing. Anyway, I just want to get done here and get back to the city."

"What's going on?" he asked.

"Nothing. There was a hot girl at the front desk."

"So do your worst. You've got a week. If you can't seduce a farmer's daughter in that length of time, you're losing your touch," Tyler said.

"She's the innkeeper's daughter, not the farmer's. And I'm pretty sure she'd shoot me on sight if I tried. She's already given me an earful about how important the factory is to the county. I figure I'll wake up to find her staging a sit-in down in the breakfast room. I'll have to listen to protest chants while I eat my oatmeal."

"Sounds like she's fiery. You always did like the difficult ones."

"Well, you were the twin who went for the easy pickings," I teased. "If it was blonde and looked at you twice, you were sold."

"That was when I valued quantity over quality. Although some of those blondes were pretty fine quality, too," he said.

"Before you start reminiscing about your greatest hits, I need to go get something to eat before the whole town closes for the evening."

I headed out to Cecil's for supper; a steak to start off the week right. And if the redhead happened to change her mind, I'd buy her a drink. If I wasn't mistaken, there was room in my brass double bed for two of us if the opportunity arose.

3

MAGGIE

"He's that hot. I mean, you'd think GQ sent him here to do a photoshoot. Short dark hair, great smile, nice ass," I said.

"So why'd you blow him off?" Sarah Jo asked. "Not that I mind coming out for a drink, but you could be here with Tall, Dark and Sexy."

"He's the Company Man. The one Hadley sent to shut down the plant. Speaking of plants, you won't be selling many of those if the factory closes, because nobody will be able to afford their water bill, much less flowers. Sarah Jo, you know how many people depend on those jobs. Since the mines shut down, you either work for the plant or your business is supported by it. Think of all the families that'll move away."

"I know. It's bad. Maybe we can convince him to keep the plant open. You should do that. You're smart, persuasive, and have great cleavage."

"Are you suggesting I offer to trade sexual favors for keeping the plant open?" I asked wryly.

"No. I'm saying if you go out with him and he really

likes you, he'll listen to you. You already said he's hot. It isn't like you don't want to anyway."

"Trust me on this one," I said. "Jeremiah Leeds is the kind of trouble I don't need."

"She means she's going to hate him in public and masturbate in private," Layla said, eating an onion ring.

Sarah Jo laughed, and I turned bright red.

"That's exactly what it means," I muttered. "He's also right over there at that table alone."

"Oh my God, that guy?" Layla asked. "You're not gonna be alone in your dirty thoughts. I've never had hate sex before, but if the corporate enemy looks like that, it might be worth a try."

"He's obviously an asshole. He is the uptight corporate dude from all those Hallmark movies," I said.

"So it's up to some adorable florist or baker or, I don't know, daycare provider, to make him fall in love with the town and save the factory!" Sarah Jo laughed.

"No thanks," I said.

"I'm asking him to join us," Sarah Jo said. "Every Hallmark movie needs a meddling friend to bring them together."

"Please don't," I begged. "I'm trying to enjoy myself tonight."

"You'll do that later," Layla wisecracked. "Just admit it. You want him to come over here so you can snark at him and get a rise out of him. In more ways than one," she teased.

"Shhh!" I hissed as Sarah Jo returned.

"He was too stuck up to hang out with us. So he's not a Hallmark hero, I guess. What can I say? A meddling friend has to try."

"Good," I said. "I never really wanted one of those bickering, opposites attract relationships anyway."

"Who said anything about a relationship?" Layla asked. "It's called a fling. You do him. A lot. You feel great, your confidence soars, he goes back home, no complications."

"I don't do that," I said.

"You're no fun," Layla complained. "If he hadn't been stuck up to Sarah Jo, I'd try the hate sex angle myself. But you know, you have first dibs."

"It's not like calling shotgun," I said with an eye roll.

"Yeah it is. You saw him first. So if you want him, go for it."

"Sarah Jo, tell her that's not who I am," I said, appealing to my more traditional friend.

"Sorry, babe, I'm with her. Go fling that sexy asshole."

We all laughed at that, but I shook my head. I did not need the kind of trouble that the swoop of desire in my stomach told me he would be.

4

JEREMIAH

The foreman and the general manager both insisted on giving me the tour of the factory and grounds. I was given a hard hat and briefed on safety procedures. The manager literally handed me the brochure they gave out to school field trip groups to explain what they did at the plant.

"You give tours? To school kids?" I asked, baffled. "Doesn't it, you know, bother them that you're killing and processing chickens? I thought kids loved cute fluffy animals."

"Nah, we give them free chicken nuggets at the end of the tour. Huge hit with the kids. Want one?" Rick, the foreman said.

"No, thank you," I said, trying not to grimace. The kids here must be a tough breed if that was their school trip—watching people process raw chicken and eating the end product as a souvenir.

"We're so glad you're here so we get to show off the plant. We're pretty proud of this here operation," Rick said. "We got some awards hanging in the office, nice plaques from the old company for safety and no accidents. Our record was 219 days without one. Then Carl Pitts fell in the vat talking on his phone. There's a reason we banned cell phones out on the floor. It's not just cause the high school co-op kids would do those stupid TikTok videos dancing around flapping pieces of raw chicken. It's a distraction. If he wouldn't have been yelling at his wife on the phone, he wouldn't have fell in the chilling vat. Damn shame about him."

"Was he killed?" I asked.

"Near enough. Broke his arm and collarbone, lungs full of that liquid—they had to do surgery after surgery and he still don't breathe quite right. We got him on office work now," he shook his head and scanned the floor sharply as if looking for anyone not doing their job.

"That's terrible," I said, wondering why he was telling me about a major industrial accident when I was inspecting to decide about shutting the place down. Not a great strategy.

"This here team does our labeling. Girls, say hello to Mr. Leeds. He's down here all the way from Hadley Corporation. Isn't it wonderful that he came all the way out here to check on us?" the foreman asked.

A line of women in paper shower caps and smocks were applying stickers to plastic packages of chicken pieces. Every label went square in the bottom left hand corner.

"Nice job, ladies. Carry on," I said.

"It's one of the plum jobs here. Everybody who's anybody in this county wants their daughter to get to be a label licker. Now the labels have adhesive on them now just like a sticker, but they used to have to lick 'em and stick 'em in the old days so we still call them the label lickers. It's an easy job, pay's good, and you don't come home stinking like scalded chicken fat," he said.

I just nodded because there was really nothing I could say to that.

"Isn't this just the best factory you ever saw?" The foreman prompted. "Look how they're on task and meeting quota!"

"Very nice, yes," I said.

As we toured the facility, I checked off the items on my list. The line was running fine. The fire exits were clear, the equipment was in working order, and people seemed to take their breaks on schedule. I made a note of it all, then the manager took me to his office.

It was wood-paneled and not very large. He had a wooden desk with a green-shaded bankers' lamp on it. It had probably been the height of style in the 1980s when the factory was built. On the wall were several plaques thanking the factory for sponsoring a blood drive or a kids' ball team, and their support for the community. As I sat down on the vinyl chair, I felt a strange surge of regret. I felt bad for this guy.

"Would you like coffee?" he asked.

"No, I'm fine. Thanks," I said. "And thank you for the tour. Rick was definitely the friendliest tour guide I've ever had."

"Rick's a terrific guy. Do you do this kind of thing a lot?"

"Inspect factories and file reports? It's part of my job. Most of the time I'm in Boston at corporate doing project management. But the head of quality control had a stroke six months ago and I was reassigned temporarily to his job."

"Do you like it?" he asked.

"That's the first time anyone's ever asked me that, Ron," I said. "No, as a matter of fact, I don't. I like planning things and figuring out the best way to make them successful. This is the opposite of that—it's evaluating someone else's work and filling out forms that show whether they're meeting objectives or not. It's a necessary evil most of the time, but it's far less constructive than what I went to college to do."

Now why had I said that? Why had I told Ron the general manager of the factory that I hated my new position and it was depressing?

"Well, then I hope you get back to your projects soon. I can't imagine a guy like you walking around with a clipboard like this all day," he said.

"I'm flattered, but I was the only man in the office qualified to carry this particular clipboard apparently," I said wryly. "Anyway, I did see your safety numbers are good, and you have a strong history of making quota. You keep your overtime within recommended limits, and your workers stay for a long time. Not much employee turnover which means you've built loyalty. You're running a good factory here, Ron," I said honestly. *Good but not great*, is what I didn't say. *Maybe not good enough for me to save it.*

"Thank you, sir," he said, "My wife'll be proud to hear it. She sets a lot of store by our performance scores. Planning on taking a cruise to the Bahamas for our twenty-fifth anniversary this year if the performance bonus stays what it was last year."

Shit. He takes pride in his work and plans to surprise his wife with a trip. Why did this have to be so goddamn human? I wanted a project to manage, a startup to expand, not a plant to shut down. It was ugly and unpleasant. Not that the guys scalding chicken carcasses had a pretty or delightful way to earn their money either.

We went over quarterly reports, and I marked off more information. He had a meeting, so I planned to speak with him again the next day.

"Before you go, I wanted to be sure and invite you to

the potluck supper tonight. A bunch of us are having a dinner to welcome you. It'll be out at the community building at six. Lots of people around here want to meet you and tell you how much this factory means to us," he said.

"A welcome dinner," I shook my head. "Well, I'd be honored."

There seemed nothing else to say considering it was the weirdest thing I ever heard. The people were so desperate to keep their factory that they were willing to pretend I was welcome there and try to win me over to their side.

I called my brother from the parking lot. "How you doing?" I asked.

"I'm good. How was your first day in Mayberry?"

"It's not Mayberry, but it's not far from it," I said ruefully. "They're having a potluck dinner for me. The whole damn town."

"Are you sure they're not trying to poison you?" he joked.

"They're so friendly and hospitable. Except for the hot girl at the front desk who rescinded her invite for orgasm queso."

"I'm going to need more information on that. Is this the one you met last night? The redhead?"

"Yes. She was flirting with me and then she took it back because I'm from corporate."

"So Hadley, in addition to transferring you from your dream job to one you hate is now a proven cockblock?" he said laughing.

"Yes," I said grimly. "And I don't see the humor in it. The curves on this woman, I swear, it's enough to make a man lose his mind."

"It sounds like you're losing yours. Over a girl you

talked to once. What's gotten into you? It's this depressing fucking job they switched you to."

"I'm sure you're right, but this depressing fucking job, as you call it, is diametrically opposed to my best interests as a man. What good are a six-figure salary and stock options when I can't get laid?"

"Maybe if you let everyone know about the money you could bag a cute gold digger," he suggested.

"I don't want a fortune hunter with tens of thousands of dollars in Botox and lip fillers for me to pay off, thanks," I said.

"Let me guess. You want real, everlasting love," he scoffed.

"There's no such thing. Just ask our mother."

"Exactly. Gather ye rosebuds while ye may, for tomorrow ye shall be knocked up," he said.

"That's a beautiful poem. You should put it in a greeting card," I quipped.

"You know I'm right. You're taking this too seriously. Have some fun. It's not like you'll ever be back that way. You can have the kind of no strings attached fling guys dream of—the kind where you have zero chance of ever running into the woman after it's over."

"So that's your dream?" I laughed. "You've disabled roadside explosive devices and secured an embassy, and your wildest dream is a one-nighter with no awkward future meeting?"

"Everyone has a dream. Some of us just don't fantasize about Super Bowl tickets or Lamborghinis."

"I'd just like a job in my field that doesn't involve destroying the dreams of entire communities."

"Okay, since when did you turn into Mr. Rogers?"

"I haven't. I've been very successful at building things,

creating projects, and expanding startups into something huge. I like that. I acknowledge the need to eliminate excessive operating costs but trashing a perfectly good factory and shoving all the workers and their families into the hole just to exploit some foreign workers—it feels shitty. I thought I was cynical enough to pull this off, but six months in and I hate it. This will be the fifth one I've shut down. The first couple it was no big deal, but it feels worse every time I have to go to a new place and do this."

"So you're up in your feelings about some chicken plant, but you're not turning into Mr. Rogers? Come on. Sing me a song about make-believe."

"Maybe if you watched more Mr. Rogers when we were kids you wouldn't be such an asshole," I said.

"You're grouchy. Cardigan too tight?" he laughed.

"You crack yourself up don't you," I groaned. "Go find yourself a job as a traveling salesman or something so you can leave town after you hook up. Go live that dream."

"I have a job. I'm doing roofing now. The money's good, and it's low stress. So don't go telling me I could do more than that. Being outside is good for me and working with my hands. I've been working out more, too. Doctor's orders."

"Your shrink told you to hit the weight room?"

"No. He told me exercise helps with the PTSD. He wants me to try yoga, but that's a little too fruity for me."

"There's hot women at yoga," I pointed out.

"I still don't know if I could do it without laughing."

"You laugh when you watch attractive women in tight leggings bend over in front of you?" I said.

"You may have a point, brother," he laughed.

Back in my room, I showered and changed. The smell of chicken processing never got more pleasant. I wondered if the workers got used to it and didn't smell it anymore, the stink of poultry and machinery and the overarching smell of scalding meat. I scrubbed with my Bulgari toiletries. I always traveled with them rather than using some flowery scented crap from a chain hotel. At this B&B they had some kind of locally sourced goat milk soap that I actually liked for my hands. I might have to go buy my mom some before I left town.

I was contemplating it while toweling off when my in-room landline phone rang. I picked it up, "Leeds here," I said, wondering who would call that phone to reach me.

"Mr. Leeds, this is Mrs. Carson. I'm sorry to disturb you, but the keys to your rental car were found in the lobby. They'll be at the front desk for you when you come down."

"Oh. Thank you," I said, looking around and realizing I must've dropped them on the way in the building. I wasn't dressed to go retrieve them, so I figured I'd get them later.

After a Skype with my direct report supervisor—a complete bastard whose answer to everything was cheap and ethically questionable relocation—I got ready for the potluck. I didn't know how to dress for a potluck dinner in a small town. I decided khakis and a button-down would be appropriate.

As I made my way down the stairs, I noticed that the redhead was at the front desk. I felt the corner of my mouth kick up involuntarily, smiling at the sight of her.

"Hey, Company Man," she said, barely looking up, "you want your keys?"

"Company Man?" I said.

"I'm sure you've been called worse," she said tartly.

"You'd be right," I said. "Thanks for the keys."

"Just one of the many services we provide here at the inn. Did you enjoy your factory tour today?"

"It was fine. Is this part of being in a small town? Everyone knows exactly what you did today?"

"I run the daycare right outside the front entrance. They're all factory kids. So their parents knew you were coming today."

"I see. Well, the tour went as well as can be expected. I did hear about a terrible accident involving a man on his cell phone—"

"I went to school with Carl Pitts. The guy's a complete dipshit. If anyone was gonna fall in a vat, it would be him, with or without the phone to distract him," she said flatly.

I couldn't help laughing, "You're very funny, you should be a comedian."

"I should look into that you know, for after you destroy our entire way of life, Company Man."

"Wow, even when you're bitchy, you're charming," I said.

"Is that like telling me I'm cute when I'm mad?" she asked.

"No. It wasn't meant to be condescending. Look, I get that you're probably angry—"

"There's no 'probably' about it. I'm angry that you're here to tell us all that the factory isn't good enough to meet your almighty corporate standard. So you can exploit the labor of the desperate and disenfranchised overseas."

"Hmm, so I take it you're not going to the welcome potluck tonight then?" I said.

"You're actually going?" she asked, looking surprised.

"Yes," I said. "It would be rude not to go."

"But not rude to close the plant?"

"That's business," I said uncomfortably. "And the people in this town are being gracious to me. While I can't be bribed, I'm not a complete asshole. I like this place. I like the goat's milk soap and the manager who wants to take his wife on a cruise. And it's inconvenient for me to start liking people here," I said. I may have sighed.

"If only you had a heart?" she teased.

"I have one. I just don't use it during working hours," I told her. "Would you like a ride to the potluck? Now that I have my rental keys back, I could give you a lift."

She shook her head, "I have to run to my parents' house first. Thank you anyway."

"You're welcome. I've honestly never been in a town where everyone was so polite."

"It's a southern thing. You're gonna like us whether you like it or not," she said.

5

MAGGIE

I'd been to dozens of potlucks at the Elks lodge. So it didn't make sense to go home and change after work and let my hair down and try to tame it. It was curly. Not the adorable Julia-Roberts-in-Pretty-Woman kind. More the Disney Princess Merida type. So it spent a lot of time in a messy bun or a very determined French braid. I had to comb it and use my overpriced spritz hair product to tame it into something more like a beachy wave and less like electric shock.

I changed into cute jeans and a top to replace my wrinkle-free and stain-resistant workwear. I got an eyelash curler and mascara involved and realized I got more dressed up for this potluck dinner than I had for my own birthday a few weeks before. Admittedly, a sheet cake at my mom's house and then margaritas at Cecil's weren't a formal evening, but I was going noticeably out of my way to look nice.

It pissed me off that I wanted to get dressed up for this guy, this stuck-up city boy Company Man sent here to ruin all our lives. He was my archenemy. I should wear shit-kicking steel toe boots and carry a pitchfork to the dinner.

But instead, I was getting pretty enough my own mama would be asking me why I was so cleaned up.

I soothed myself by remembering the part of Wonder Woman where she wears the kick-ass blue ball gown with a sword on her back. Pretty can be tough, I told myself. It's a kind of armor. It's the way I was brought up—be pretty and sweet and polite, don't disagree, just coax. I had never been good at that crap. I was good with kids, with silly rhymes and songs and loving them all and helping them understand they were still loved even when they had to go to time-out. And nobody was going to take that from me.

At my parents' house, I picked up the potato casserole I was contributing to the dinner.

"Thanks for heating it up for me," I said, "you all ready?"

"We're gonna head up there in a few minutes. You look mighty pretty tonight, Maggie," my mother said suspiciously.

"Just felt like dressing up a little. My wrinkle-free khakis and my cartoon t-shirts are fine for work, but sometimes a girl could use a break from the Buzz and Woody shirts," I made an excuse.

"Are you sure this has nothing to do with that horrible man from Hadley? Because he looks just like that actor you used to have posters of when you were in school."

"What actor?" I said, as if I didn't know.

"The one from Hunger Games, the dark-headed one."

"Liam Hemsworth. And no, this guy does not look like Liam Hemsworth," I said a little too vehemently.

"Really?" she cocked a knowing eyebrow at me. I shrugged.

"I'll see you there," I said, avoiding the question.

He did look like Gale, my crush from the Hunger Games movies. I never liked the sweet baker boy in those. I liked the competitive, hotheaded guy who was tall, dark and dangerous. Except this guy was here in town, looking wicked and being the kind of adversary that made my mouth water. He was real, and he was a danger to my town. There was also a slight but serious risk that I'd drop my panties for him if he asked.

I took my casserole to the Elks lodge, determined to leave with my dignity and my panties right where they belonged. I got there with the first wave of people and helped them set up. Layla was fussing over her bourbon balls, arranging them in circles on a glass plate, "Is a target pattern too obvious?" she asked.

"Nah," I said. "He knows we hate him. Just as long as you don't use him for actual target practice, it should be fine."

"You don't look like you hate him. You're lusting. Tell me you took the edge off with your battery-powered boyfriend, because if not, you may not survive the night," she said.

"I don't know what you're talking about. Maybe you tasted too much bourbon while you were cooking."

"Unlike you, the only balls I'm interested in here are on this plate. If you want him, go get him. I'm all for it. But you look half-crazed."

"Only half? Payton had a tantrum in the toddler room today that could've gone viral as an exorcism if we'd filmed it."

"So what's different about that? You work with kids. They're like wild animals—moody and unpredictable."

"If that makes them wild animals, then you're one, too," I said.

"You're not wrong," she said, licking powdered sugar off

her thumb, "look who's here. It's the man of the hour."

My head whipped around as I checked out the door. There he was, dressed like a model in a J. Crew catalog. I wanted to get down on my knees and bite the neat row of buttons off his striped shirt. My face heated at the thought. Layla disappeared, then came right back and handed me a plastic cup of sweet tea.

"Here, drink this. You're looking thirsty," she said with a snort.

"You walked all the way across the room to make that joke," I said. "Sad."

"Like you noticed. You never took your eyes off him. You look like you could eat him alive, which I guess is one way to get him to save the factory."

"I'm not giving out blow jobs for business favors."

"I'm not suggesting it at all. I'm saying that factory's worth hundreds of thousands of dollars in wages to this town if not more. And if a well-timed sexual favor saved that, it would be a heroic act."

"So you *are* suggesting it."

"Never. I'm saying if it was me, and it was something I wanted to do anyway..."

"So you're saying I should blow him and then demand he keep the plant open?"

"We've had worse ideas."

"Like the time I let you talk me into cutting bangs? It took me a year and a half to grow that out. It was a nightmare. So if I don't take advice from you, don't get your feelings hurt. I love you, but your ideas suck."

"Maybe if you sucked, we could keep the factory," she said with a laugh.

"God, you're the worst," I laughed, elbowing her.

I went to help set out plastic silverware and pour some drinks. The sweet tea hadn't cooled me down a bit.

Sarah Jo and Luke were there setting out burgers and wings Cecil's was contributing, and Macy from the bakery was putting her special frosted cookies on a fancy tiered tray that looked like it belonged at an afternoon tea. I went over and said hi, so glad the town was coming out in force to try and win Jeremiah over.

"How's your dad?" I asked Sarah Jo.

"He's good. He finally settled in to the assisted living over in Pendleton close to Ryan, and he likes it there. Says the food's better than my cooking."

"That's got to be a load off your mind," I said, "and I'm glad Ryan stepped up."

"Well," she said, her voice dropping to a whisper, "he quit drinking, and it's made a world of difference."

"Really? What finally got him to stop?"

"I'm not sure. I wish I knew who it was. I'd give them free queso and margaritas for life," Sarah Jo said.

About that time, Macy from the bakery dropped one end of her huge white box of cookies and some tumbled out onto the floor. We dove for them, saving the ones that didn't break while she apologized and tried to salvage what was left.

"Thank you," she said. "I'm so clumsy."

"That box is huge, and besides, everybody drops stuff," I said, "it's great that you brought these. They're so pretty."

"I'm just happy that people like them," she said. "If they didn't, I might end up eating them all by myself."

"When I was pregnant, I would go get a dozen of them for the shop, and I'd eat four or five of them myself," Sarah Jo said.

"I've eaten five in a row, and I'm not pregnant," Luke

said. "They're just that good."

"Thank you," she said, looking shy.

Macy went back to her cookie display, and I scanned the room for Jeremiah Leeds. He was across the room from me, hands in his pockets, looking for all the world like he didn't know what in hell he was doing there.

He went to the little wood podium and raised the microphone to his height, "Excuse me, everyone. I just wanted to thank you all for coming tonight and for hosting this dinner. It's very kind of you," he cleared his throat and seemed a little stiff. "Everything looks delicious. Please, go ahead and start the meal."

He stepped back, nearly plowing into Rev. Mark who was going to say the grace. I noticed Jeremiah bowed his head but seemed unsure what to do. After everyone said Amen, people started lining up to fill their plates. I set down the napkins I was carrying, tossed my careful waves off my shoulder and stood up straight. I was going to do battle. Just verbal sparring, just coaxing him to love my town, maybe a little flirting. Nothing too dangerous. Except with him, I could tell it was all too dangerous. I felt a thrum of excitement in my body as my heartbeat kicked up.

The mayor had sidelined him and was talking, gesturing with his hands. Jeremiah was nodding, but he seemed a little taken aback. I went to join them. I breezed right up to them and slipped my hand into his elbow. I meant to be cheerful and welcoming, but the galvanic shock that jolted through me at the touch seemed to shred my ability to use words. I almost pulled my hand away from his arm, but his heavy bicep felt too good to let go. I wanted to use my grip on his arm to turn him to face me and kiss him, hot and hungry. I wanted his hands on me, demanding and taking. The heat in his eyes as they met mine turned my body to something molten, something that longed to surrender to him. I could easily imagine him hauling me against him, claiming my mouth, his muscled chest hard against my aching breasts.

"Good evening, Maggie," the mayor said, pulling me from my thoughts.

"Good evening, sir," I said with a smile. "You don't mind if I borrow the guest of honor, do you? I thought it would be rude if we didn't let him fill his plate pretty soon. All those tamales your wife makes will go fast, and we don't want him to miss out on those."

"Oh, you're sweet to say so. They sure are a hit around our house. The grandkids love 'em. You two go right ahead. I'll talk to you later," he said. "Good meeting you."

"Yes, sir, thank you," Jeremiah said, more respectfully than I expected.

We started away from the mayor, "What?" Jeremiah said.

"What?" I said back.

"You just looked shocked."

"I was—you were polite to the mayor, and I guess I was surprised."

"My mother taught us manners, in case you thought I was raised by wolves."

"I shouldn't have assumed you'd be rude to him."

"No, you shouldn't. Am I such a monster?"

"Maybe, or maybe not. I haven't decided yet," I said, smiling at him just because I enjoyed his arm under my hand and the warm citrus smell of him and the sound of his voice. I'd like to have that voice say my name, would like to have those hands of his make me beg for more. I swallowed hard, trying to remember this was business. The business of saving my town. Pleasure couldn't enter into it.

6

JEREMIAH

There she was at my side, urging me to try a little of the mac and cheese from the diner, the burger from Cecil's, Mrs. May's salad 'the good kind with nuts and strawberries in it'. She told me who made everything. There were four long tables lined with food, and she could identify every dish and its origin like some archaeologist. Everything she said was entertaining, colorful. But she'd glance up at me and look a little concerned. Like I was going to say something obnoxious in response.

"Am I that fearsome?" I said.

Maggie had just told me that the carrot and raisin salad was the minister's mother's specialty, that she still used her mother's World War II ration book recipe. Then she looked at me, a wrinkle between her brows.

"What?"

"Every time you tell me something interesting, you look at me like you anticipate a bad reaction from me."

"I just keep expecting you to say something about cutesy small towns and how we're so backwoods or something."

"Have I said anything like that at all?" I asked. "Or have you got me confused with somebody you saw in a movie?"

She just looked at me.

"I mean I'm not going to treat you like you just walked off the Beverly Hillbillies if you'll quit looking at me like I'm some heartless corporate villain from a movie."

"What kind of movie has the Beverly Hillbillies and a corporate villain?" she asked dubiously. "I would watch the hell out of that."

I laughed. "I'm not judging your community just because it's different from the city."

"No, you're just going to eat our potato casserole and then shut down the factory anyway," I said a little petulantly.

"Is this your casserole?"

"Yes," she said.

"So tell me something interesting about the cook. You have for everything else."

"Let's see..." she said, thinking it over. "my favorite color is blue, I love my mama's biscuits and gravy, and I don't want to lose the business I worked so hard to create to go up in smoke when you shut down the factory."

"Maggie—" I started.

"What? You don't like my list? I'm very interesting, don't you think?""

"You left something out."

"What?"

"Are you seeing anyone?" I asked. She frowned at me. An actual frown, not a fleeting look of displeasure. Then she shook her head.

"No. I'm not."

"You're not?"

"No. No boyfriend. Unless you count Garrett."

"Who's Garrett?" I said.

"He wants to marry me," she said, with a half-smile. "But he's a little young for me."

"How old?"

"He's four. Real charmer though. Blue eyes, can put on his own shoes if they're Velcro," she laughed. I couldn't help laughing too.

"Well, what more can you want in a man than that?" I said.

"It's my Bumble profile. Female seeking male who can put on shoes, tying not necessary."

"I've seen worse profiles," I said.

"What? No way do you do dating apps."

"I have. I travel a lot for my job, which makes it difficult to meet someone in my home base," I said simply.

"So I'm supposed to be too mature to make a dirty joke about getting to third base here, right?"

"Exactly. I find it challenging to meet women I'd be interested in. I meet people everywhere, of course, and I have no objection to a long-distance relationship, but I haven't found a woman who made me worry I'd regret leaving her behind."

"Well, that sounds pretty callous," she said, scooping more potatoes onto my plate for me. "These are really good. You'll thank me."

"What about you?"

"I have a plate. See?" she said, showing me her piled-up plate of food.

"I mean why aren't you seeing someone?"

"I'll tell you what I tell my mom. Apps don't work when you grew up with every guy in a twenty-mile radius. Let's face it, if I saw you picking your nose at the football games in high school, I'm just not gonna be attracted to you as adults."

"So the profile gets longer. Female seeks male who can put on shoes. No nose pickers. That's going to narrow the field considerably," I teased.

"I'm a woman who deserves the best. Plus, I deal with enough nose pickers at work. Probably the thing I say most besides, "Do you need to potty?" is "Get your fingers out of there!" she said.

I laughed, "That could apply to a lot of things, not just the nose."

"Ha-ha," she said flatly, "Little boys stick their hands down their pants. I've noticed. We just say, that's not something we do at school, and then we go wash hands."

"Sounds like a winning strategy. So you don't have to add 'keeps hands out of own pants' to your list. You're already prepared to deal with that if it happens," I said, stifling a laugh.

"Yes. I have skills," she said, nibbling a dinner roll and balancing her plate. We made our way to a table covered with purple and green plastic tablecloths and set our plates down on it.

"Mardi Gras?" I asked.

"School colors," she clarified. "We're the Cougars."

"And cougars are purple and green?" I said dubiously.

"'Round here they are. We are the purple and green, best that you've ever seen—" she cheered, ending with two claps and her arms outstretched.

"You were a cheerleader?" I said.

"No way. But I went to games, so I know the cheers. Lots of school spirit around here. The basketball team went to regionals three years ago. We lost in game one, but it was an exciting time."

"Okay," I said, taking a bite of my burger. It was very good, and I said so.

"Yeah, Cecil's is great. My friend Sarah Jo is married to the owner's son, Luke. He's on the fire department. Those ribs are from Jake, my friend Cat's cousin. He's another fireman. He's got his own meat smoker and does the best turkeys at Thanksgiving. And that cookie you have there, Macy down at the grocery store bakery counter makes those. They're amazing."

"So everyone's related here," I said.

"No. We just all know each other. It's nice. Everywhere you go somebody asks how you're doing, asks about your family. We look out for each other."

"Is that what this is?" I bristled. "You looking out for them? Is that why you rescued me from the mayor's lecture?"

"Not entirely. I admit that part of me wants to be the one to convince you to save the plant. I wouldn't mind showing off like that. Being the hero. Not the way Layla suggested though."

"Oh, really, the one with the overalls? What was her idea? Get me a cowboy hat and some boots?" I said.

"Blow job," she deadpanned.

I choked on my potatoes. I coughed and hacked. She handed me a napkin and I coughed into it, eyes watering, swigging water in desperation.

"What?" I croaked between coughs.

"Blow. Job. It's where someone uses their mouth—" she had a mischievous glint in her eyes.

"Stop," I said, cutting her off. It felt like a brushfire had just engulfed my body, from the soles of my feet all the way through my hardening cock and straight up to the tips of my ears.

She laughed, a big, glorious sound and slapped her thigh.

"I'm familiar with the concept. I've had one. I mean, more than one," I said. How did this small-town girl catch me off guard and leave me stammering?

"You should see your face," she said.

"You'll have to forgive me if I react when someone, particularly an attractive woman, uses the phrase blow job in dinner conversation."

"Are you city boys so traditional? Should I put on an apron and go refill your tea glass?" she said.

"No. I'm not like that. I was startled. And when I talk to you, everything seems to come out wrong."

She flashed me a dazzling smile.

She was just screwing with me. I knew by the wicked grin on her face. And I loved it.

"So your friend thought you should trade a blow job for the factory staying open?"

"Yes and no. She's not a pimp or anything. It was a joke."

"I see," I said. "My brother and I have similar conversations. Hilarious ones that anyone else would think was insane."

"You have a brother?"

"A twin, in fact. He's home from the Marines, working in construction now."

"A twin? How cool. Were you super close growing up?" she said, genuinely interested.

"Sometimes. And sometimes we beat the crap out of each other. He makes me better. I like to think I do the same for him."

"How so?" she said.

"Well, when he decided to enlist, he spent that whole

summer working out. I was never into that, but I have this competitive streak, especially when it comes to him. I didn't want to be the scrawny twin. So I started hitting the gym, too. He was my motivation to prove I was as good as he was."

"I can see how you'd be compared a lot," she said thoughtfully.

"Yes. It's a great motivator, for me, at least. What about you? What's your motivation? Besides defeating me and saving your town?"

"I've always wanted to do something bigger, I guess. Something that helps a lot of people."

"Well, you're educating kids. That's big."

"Yes, but it's not all. I opened a daycare because I saw a need. Mrs. Susan, who ran the daycare downtown for years was retiring, and I knew there would be a bunch of preschoolers with no place to go while their parents worked. So I did my licensing, took the classes, reached the goal of opening before Susan closed her doors. That way I was in place, and her staff and students had a place to be."

"That's very civic-minded of you."

"I enjoy it. I enjoy running my own business, having no one to answer to. I like the kids and the people I work with. I've got the place open sixteen hours a day running on two shifts with part-timers covering lunch breaks. First shift starts at six-thirty so I open at six."

"You're a go-getter. You could close up here and go to the city and make a success of your business, I'm sure."

"Who said I'm not successful already?" she asked. "Besides, for better or worse, I live here. It's the only place I ever wanted to be. So I'm staring down the barrel of shuttering the place. If you chain the gate on that plant, it takes me and mine down with it."

"I'm sure you have clients who aren't employed at the factory," I hedged, feeling uncomfortably like I was here to eat her potatoes and ruin her life.

"Three. I have two students whose mom works at the city water department and one whose mom works at the convention center in Pendleton but lives here in town."

"That's a small percentage," I said, feeling deflated.

It was the strangest feeling. I was uncomfortable with the topic of conversation, but I wanted to spend more time with Maggie. I should have wanted to get away, but instead, I wanted to pull her close. "I'm used to towns practically coming at me with pitchforks and torches. So being welcomed here is unusual to say the least. I know that this plant is extremely valuable to your community. A lot of jobs hinge on this, and other businesses depend on the factory as well, like yours. I didn't set out to make enemies."

"But you have. That doesn't mean we can't be friendly, though. This is the South after all. So as long as you're not William Tecumseh Sherman back from the dead, we'll still serve you tea and offer you another helping of dessert. Speaking of which, did you try my mama's deep-dish apple pie?"

"No. Is that a real change of subject or are you trying to poison me?"

"That's me, Company Man. I'm the Wicked Queen."

Her sly smile gave the throwaway phrase a filthy weight that hung in the air between us.

"If you're going to insist on calling me by that nickname, I guess I'll call you Wicked Queen in return," I said.

"Your Majesty will do just fine," she said.

"I think I'll pass on the pie, Your Majesty," I joked. "Because I already ate a heaping plate of, I think, every-thing. It was very good. And kind of everyone to do this. I've seen some factory people here that I should go speak to. I don't want them to feel that I'm avoiding them or that a decision has already been made," I said. "If you'll excuse me."

"Yes, of course," she said.

In a few minutes' time, a band started to play. People shuffled onto the floor, old married couples, a few teenagers with braces and Save the Turtles t-shirts on. Some twangy country song played, and instead of wincing as I usually would at the cheesy music, I searched Maggie out. I wasn't just there for the potluck and to build goodwill for Hadley. It seemed more and more like I was here for Maggie Carson.

I made my way to her, stood at her elbow while she finished talking. I didn't even say anything. The air between us was thick with promise, with unspoken lust and something more. So when I reached down and took her hand as casually as she'd taken my arm earlier, the sparks shouldn't have surprised me. It was a raw jolt of energy passing between us, not the kind of shock you get from scuffing across the carpet and touching the doorknob, but a deep sizzle of fiery connection that set my nerves on edge and made me want her mouth all over me. In the length of time I took for me to take her hand in mine and to look her in the eyes with my unspoken request, I had blinked my eyes twice. Both times in the space between heartbeats I had seen a vision of myself with my head between her legs, the two of us in a car, her legs splayed, thighs parted around my face as my hungry mouth worked her. I got so hard at the thought that it was difficult to walk normally as we made our way onto the makeshift dance floor.

The music slid into a slow song, and the floor grew

crowded. I slid my arm around her waist. Her fingers curved behind my neck. I held her left hand in my right, her fingers small in my palm. Some ancient Garth Brooks song piped through the static-rattled amp. Just like that, I was holding her. When she looked up into my eyes, her long eyelashes fluttered as she looked down and away a little shyly. The same brash woman from the registration desk, the woman whose smart mouth and gorgeous body had kept me hard for damn near a full day was bashful in my arms. That felt like a spike of electricity in my blood. I wondered what else she might do, what other moods struck her. Brazen, sassy, shy, serious—I wanted every color of her, every mood, every expression.

Not electricity in my blood, on second thought. She was more like heroin, sharp and dizzying and making me want more.

"Maggie," I said.

"Mm-hmm?" she said, looking back up at me.

"I like dancing with you," I said.

She grinned, "Me, too. I mean, you're the enemy obviously. But enemies can dance can't they?"

"Oh, I'd say enemies could do a lot of things. I'm sure you've heard about keeping your enemies closer."

"I have. Exactly how close are you suggesting?" she said, a teasing purr in her voice that went straight to my cock.

I cleared my throat, "That depends on how close you're interested in being."

Just then, the song ended, and some loud Skynard cover started to blast. We stepped away from each other, nearly staggering. The spell was broken, that sultry hush between us when we'd danced.

Greedy, I wanted to pull her back into my arms, maybe

bend her head back over my arm while I kissed her thoroughly, plundering that pretty mouth with my tongue. I shoved my hands in my pockets, feeling irritable and keyed up. Just that taste of her in my arms, not even a kiss—it had been intoxicating.

"You know, Company Man," she said ruefully, "This isn't going to turn out like a Hallmark movie."

"I have no idea what you're talking about."

"This can't happen. Anything with you and me. We're on opposite sides of a fight, and I have too much at stake to put that aside. No matter how much I liked dancing with you."

"I understand," I said, "And I have a job to do. No matter how beautiful you are or how funny you are."

"No need to flatter me," she said.

"I'm not," I countered. "You can't tell me I'm the first man to call you beautiful?"

"No, not the first. But it's been a while," she admitted.

"Then everybody in this town is too nearsighted to know what's in front of them. Jesus, look at you."

I touched her fiery, wavy hair, winding one long curl around my index finger and releasing it, watching it unwind. It was intimate, the slide of that auburn twist of silken hair around my skin.

"I shouldn't want you as much as I do."

"I know," she said, her eyes never leaving mine.

I was still touching her hair, threading my fingers through it, surprised at how heavy it was, how springy to the touch like a live thing. I couldn't stop touching it. She took another step toward me, as if she didn't want me to stop.

"So I'm not getting involved. I'm here to do my job," I said, my voice sounding far away.

"Right. And there's no way I'd go out with someone who's looking to shut down the plant and take my daycare down with it," she said, swallowing hard.

The air between us was hot and alive. Her eyes locked on mine, unwavering, and my hand in her hair. All of it said something different from our words. I felt her shiver at my touch when my fingertips brushed her scalp. I couldn't resist. I raked my fingers through her hair, palmed her head in my hand. I watched her lips part at the sensation, at the bone-deep knowledge that I was going to kiss her. That she wanted it, too. I let my gaze drift to her rosy, parted lips. I watched the rise and fall of her chest as she breathed heavily, anticipating my mouth on hers. When I drew her a step closer to me, she stumbled, her hand going to my chest. Her palm, the spread of her fingers seared into my flesh as if they burned my shirt away. I felt branded, taken in a way I never had before. I wondered if my hand in her hair felt the same way to her. I heard my own breath sawing in and out like I'd been running. The tip of her pink tongue peeked out as she wetted her lips.

I let go of her, withdrew my hand and stepped back smoothly. The almost kiss was the most intense caress of my life. I knew from the way she looked at me that she'd felt every stroke of my tongue as surely as if I had really kissed her.

"I'm not wasting our first kiss in a roomful of people," I said. "Nothing against the Elk's lodge."

She nodded, "Right."

"I'll see you again soon."

She nodded her agreement and went to join her friends without another word. I watched her walk away, enjoying the sight of her and the way she moved. But for some reason, I felt like I was left with flaming tire tracks up my back when she walked away. That woman was invested in the factory. I had a job to do. But there was no earthly reason why I couldn't have some fun while I was in town. Fun that felt like it would burn down the world.

7

MAGGIE

"So that was inconvenient," I told my sister, Ella.

"What was?" she asked on our weekly phone call.

"They sent a hot guy to shut down the chicken factory."

"He isn't hot. You're wrong. You're just lonely. Get yourself a new pack of batteries and get this out of your system. A man who comes to town to close our only major industry has no right to be attractive. You are not attracted to him. You just miss having a boyfriend."

"I don't miss having a boyfriend, and I'm not horny. Or it's not *just* that. He's seriously attractive and charming. I haven't been this attracted to anyone since—ever. And of course, it has to be fucking Ebenezer Scrooge or whatever because I couldn't be attracted to a nice normal guy. It had to be my archenemy."

"You got a cape now? Who has an archenemy in real life?"

"Trust me, El, if some dude is closing the plant and your job is collateral damage, he's your archenemy."

"I'm not saying he isn't THE enemy. But how his he yours specifically?"

"Because. My daycare relies on the plant employees' business. So he's de facto attacking my livelihood as well as the well-being of my entire community."

"De facto, huh?" she laughed. "Serious shit if you're going Latin."

"You have to see what a huge deal this is."

"I get it. The town is going to suffer hugely. People will move out in droves. Your business and countless others will fold, and most of the working class will have to relocate."

"No, not that. The sexiness thing!" I said. "That's the problem."

"Gee, sis, I'm confused. I thought the devastating effect of unemployment on thousands of people was the issue. But you have pants feelings for the bad guy, so I guess I missed the point here."

"You are such a smartass. The conversation is about me and my problems. You don't have problems on account of being perfect."

"I've gained three pounds."

"So what, you're a size two now?" I laughed. "Try praying your eights will zip, and we'll talk weight gain sometime."

"You're the curvy one. I got no boobs to speak of. I'd take a little junk in the trunk if I had boobs," Ella moaned.

"Well, I'd trade you my rack right now to get rid of this vibe I have going with the Company Man," I groaned back.

"Vibe? Okay, I'm going to need details," she said.

"Like, eye contact with him feels sexual, like no one else is in the room and it's something private."

"So dirty eye contact? Really? Are you sure he doesn't have a nervous tic or something?"

"He does not have a tic. It's just intense. At the potluck, we were talking and laughing, it was easy and fun but there was this chemistry all over the place just zinging around. It felt like, you know, when you wake up with a really good hair day, you find twenty bucks in your coat pocket you didn't know was there, everybody's in a good mood, and the boots you wanted are on half price. Like everything was right with the world."

"I don't think I've ever had a day like that, much less a guy who makes me feel that way. Wait, is it like the Pilates feeling? Like that happy rush of well-being after a really tough Pilates class?" she said.

"You're so healthy it makes me want to throw up," I said. "I have no idea, since I've never done Pilates. But everything feels great and easy and happy with him. Which is horrible, because he's like the bringer of doom."

"Oooh—Doombringer the Grim, that's a great D&D name!"

"Tell me you're not still dating the guy who does gaming. I mean, when you said he was into role playing I assumed you had to wear a French maid outfit or something, not like barbarians and overlords and shit."

"We're not together, no. But the game was so fun that I still go by and play at least once a month."

"You're too nice. I would've thrown all his weird ass cards and games and shit away when he cheated on me. Sent him the ashes in a box."

"That's why you're never friends with your exes, babe," she said.

"True, but I'm okay with that. And, look, the thing with Jeremiah—"

"You mean Company Man? Do *not* start thinking of him by his name, he's a problem, not a potential boyfriend. Put that out of your mind right now."

"I know," I said, crestfallen.

"Oh, come on. Have a fling, woman! Jeez, I can't believe you bought that for a second from me. Seize your happiness, get laid, I don't care about his job! If you feel the chemistry, and he's hot and it's fun, then what's not to enjoy? It's not marriage. It's just a roll in the hay."

"Thank goodness. I thought you were getting all traditional on me," I said with relief.

"Seriously, you need to get laid. And if the guy shutting down the factory is who does it for you, go ahead. You know I support anything that makes you happy."

"I love that about you, El, but the fact is, I don't think it would make me happy. I'd be miserable knowing I was sleeping with the enemy. On the other hand—every time I so much as lay eyes on him, it feels like something sexual has to happen between us. I'm so keyed up, and my whole body gets hot all over, and I just want him to—do things to me. Things I haven't done with anyone else."

"Does he feel the same way about you?" she said.

"That's the big question. We danced at the potluck. We almost kissed. He seemed interested."

"Yeah, he wants to stick it in you."

I laughed as we said our goodbyes and promised to update her if anything happened with Jeremiah.

A little holiday, a break from being so responsible didn't sound like such a bad thing. I felt giddy at the idea.

I trotted upstairs and rapped on his door.

"Hey," I said, feeling a bubbly nervousness, "do you want to go get a drink?"

He stood there in his doorway, looking handsome as hell, that heat coming off his skin that I seemed to feel and respond to even two feet away.

"Yes, absolutely. Where would you like to go?"

This was going to be fun.

8

JEREMIAH

I did not expect to see her at my door. I figured I'd spend the evening calling my brother, doing some work, answering emails. Maybe crack open the airplane bottle of vodka in my suitcase and watch some ESPN. So a beautiful redhead offering to go out for a drink was an upgrade over what I had planned.

I was startled, thrilled, a little confused. I wanted to go right that second before she changed her mind, but I was barefoot.

"Come on in. I have to get ready," I said.

She stepped into the room and a hundred things flashed through my head. All of them X-rated. I wanted her in that room. But I didn't want to spend my time looking for my socks and shoes.

"Make yourself at home," I said tightly, trying to ignore my body's response to her. Instead of a commonplace 'wait a second while I get my shoes on' interaction, this felt fraught with sexual tension.

My pulse seemed to beat in my neck, my fingertips. I

hastily shoveled through my once-organized bag to find clean socks.

"I *am* at home here, always have been. I'm the one who put the sheets on that bed before you arrived because the housekeeper was running late. I used to play in the empty rooms. Especially the bathrooms. Every tub in this place hosted a Barbie pool party at one time or another," she said lightly.

I smiled at that. She was so at ease with herself here, not in the room of a strange man, but in a room of her second home where she'd grown up. She lounged on a club chair, its country-looking floral pattern suddenly old-fashioned and pretty framing her hair and complexion. I got myself together and opened the door for her to precede me.

"Lead the way."

We had said very little, but the sparks between us, the smiles that seemed private—it was its own conversation. My hand brushing the small of her back as we went out to the car.

"We can walk," she said, so I pocketed my keys. We walked the few blocks to Cecil's. I wanted to reach for her hand, but it seemed too loaded with meaning or something. Like it would be me claiming her. Everything felt like I was ready to claim her. Every action had weight; every look was so full of intensity. We said a few words. I mentioned how pretty the town was, how kind everyone had been.

"That must make your job harder," she said.

"Yes, it does. But I'm surprised you said so. Considering why I'm here."

"I don't have to like your job to realize it's not an easy thing. This is hard for all of us," she said. It struck me as such a fair thing to say, so generous under the circumstances.

"I'm going to assume since you're so understanding that you're not going to get me drunk and threaten to post videos of me acting like an idiot, so I'll keep the factory open," I said. As soon as I said it, I felt crappy about it. It was an obnoxious thing to say especially after she'd been so mature.

"We'll see. It's an idea," she said playfully.

We sat down at a table and ordered our drinks. She insisted I try the queso there, which really was delicious.

"I haven't had chips and dip in I don't know how long," I mused.

"Why not?"

"That's a good question. I don't know. I guess I just never think to buy them for myself."

"Hmmm. They're like the first thing on my list," she said.

"Ahhh so you should add chip connoisseur to your titles along with desk clerk and teacher," I teased.

"I'm not a teacher. I mean I have the credentials for early childhood ed, but I'm the director of the facility. It's more the business side than the teaching side. I like it, running my own business, making all the decisions, knowing I can make it come out right. I mean, my parents own their own business so there's some control thing there for me, and I like being my own boss."

"I understand. I want that someday myself. I'm good at what I do, or at what I did before I was reassigned. I was a project manager. I could turn an idea into something practical and profitable, and bigger than they ever imagined. That's what I like to do," I said almost wistfully.

"So tearing businesses apart and shutting them down isn't your idea of a good time?" she asked sarcastically.

"No, it's not. I see that it's necessary sometimes, but it's not my dream job."

"So you didn't sit on the plane sharpening your claws for the kill or anything?" she joked.

"No, not at all. "

"Good, and I wasn't brewing poison apples in a cauldron to get rid of you."

"No, you were just standing behind the registration desk like a thirst trap."

"Oh really?" she said, grinning hugely at the compliment.

"Really."

"And I thought you were inconvenient."

"Was I interrupting something?" I said, leaning into the heavy flirting, the flush on her cheeks and the ripe plummy lips I wanted to capture.

"My life. You interrupted my life," she said lightly, but her voice was lower, like she was sharing a secret. "I was ready to hate you and try to run you out of town. Then you walked in looking so hot, that close-cropped dark hair and the wicked smile."

"So my smile is wicked?" I said, giving her a half smile I hoped would make her clothes practically fall off.

"Very," she said, a little breathless.

The breathlessness was a victory. I wanted to roar with triumph and claim my prize right then and there. I wanted to take her chin in my hand and kiss her till she was begging for air. She would beg. I would make her want me so much. My mouth watered for her. I wanted to cup her mound, finger her through her clothes and feel her hot and wet, creaming herself for me. Then I'd give it to her, fast and slick and sweaty right up against the wall of my room. I'd pound her so hard the walls would shake, and she'd plead for more. I could feel it between us in the itch of my palms, the way she already starred in every fantasy I had, the filthier the better.

"You know, I have a policy about mixing business with pleasure," I said.

"Did you learn it by watching reruns of Dallas from the 80's?" she said.

"No, I don't chase secretaries around the desk. I don't even call mine a secretary."

"How modern of you," she said. "So what's the policy?"

"It's more of a rule. I think mixing business and pleasure is a threat to integrity. It can cloud the judgment."

"So which one am I? Business or pleasure?" she asked.

"You're both. I'd be a fool to pretend that my business here in town didn't have a direct impact on you and your daycare center. So I'm not overlooking that. I'm saying I want to know you better, spend time with you. Break my own rules."

We talked and laughed. I enjoyed her quirky sense of humor, her full and joyful laugh. I reached over once and touched her hair. The same way I had at the dinner when we danced, the coil of ruddy silk twisted around my finger, gripped and let loose to curl free against the curve of her cheek. I heard the game commentary end on the big screen TV's and glanced at the clock. It was eleven. We both had work, so it was time to break up the party. I was reluctant to say anything. In fact, just as I was getting ready to tell her I'd had a nice time, but we should go, I reached for her hand instead.

I could get addicted to the soft fingers in my palm, the way her skin tasted of vanilla cream when I kissed the spot between her thumb and forefinger. I had kissed her hand quite naturally, not even realizing it. She glanced around as if to see if anyone was looking while color stole up her neck to set her cheeks blazing.

"Would you like to come up to my room?"

"I've seen your room. I put the sheets on that bed, remember?" she quipped.

"And this would give you a chance to try them out, make sure they're comfortable enough for your guests," I said pointedly. She bit her lip and shook her head.

"I think I'd better not," she said.

"All right. It was still a nice evening. If you'll let me, I'll drive you home."

"I'd like that," she said as we walked back to the B&B where my rental was still parked.

I captured her hand as I drove. Her sweet vanilla scent seemed to fill the air around me, drowning out the generic air freshener the rental company had sprayed inside. She filled the space, her laugh and the sight and fragrance of her. I wanted her beyond reason. She had said no. I understood that, and for tonight, it was a no. That didn't mean there wasn't any tomorrow or another chance.

"I hope I didn't insult you when I asked you to spend the night with me."

"You didn't."

"Just not that kind of girl?" I said archly.

"Yeah, that's me. The good girl," she joked. I could still tell she was uncomfortable, so I dropped the subject.

"Where do I turn?" I said after a minute.

"You're gonna want to take a left at that corner and it's the little white one with the deep porch."

"The one with a chimney on each side?" I said. "I love that one."

"You do? I mean, you. Mr. Brooks Brothers designer preppy loves my old house? It's painted brick. It has a drafty original fireplace with bookcases on each side and the floor slants a little to the east. I just can't imagine someone so GQ liking something so down-home."

"Maybe there's more to me than meets the eye, Maggie," I said, "and you'll have to discover it."

"Thank you for the ride. And for being a gentleman."

"I asked you to spend the night with me. That's not a gentleman, at least not in the sense I understand it."

"You didn't give me any shit about turning you down. You didn't act like I owe you something."

"You don't. We'd have a good time together. Unforgettable, in fact. But not tonight. We barely know each other, and you're not comfortable with that. Maybe it's my job, or my cologne. Whatever it is, it's your business. It doesn't make me want you less. So being an ass about it would materially reduce my chances in the future."

"Always the businessman," she laughed, but there was relief in her voice, too.

"Since I'm posing as a gentleman tonight, let me open your door for you."

I got out of the car and opened her door for her. She stepped out. Her full height was perfect, petite and curvy and the top of her head just below my chin.

I looked down at her and caught her gaze. It was dark with want and her eyes were hooded with heavy lids.

I ran my hands down her arms, took her hands in mine and held them. Then I laid her hands on my shoulders and took her in my arms, everything in hot, syrupy slow motion. Our eyes locked in the dim light from her porch as I dipped my head and my lips rubbed against hers. Just a sensuous rub, feeling the soft, plump texture of her yielding lips, how eager and sweet they tasted. I caught her bottom lip between mine and tugged just a little, locking lips with her, going slow. She raised up on tiptoe to get closer, her arms winding around my neck.

As I parted her lips, unhurried, in control of the kiss, I stole her breath. I felt that gasp, took the gasp into my own body as if to keep it forever. She took my tongue into her mouth with a sigh that seemed so satisfied that I hardened even more at the sound. I was giving her strokes of my tongue along hers, learning the curves of her mouth, and I was giving her exactly what she wanted.

This kiss seemed to go on forever, stoking the passion between us as I struggled, my iron control slipping. It was supposed to be a light, good night kiss, a sipping at her lips to taste her but not a deep, sexual drink. No matter how I tried to hold back, some primal instinct drew me in, pulled me down into darkness as my passion unleashed. I gripped her face, plundered her mouth with my tongue, felt the way her body loosened, opened for me. My knee pushed between her open thighs, giving her pressure where she wanted it. She rocked a little against my leg. When she did, that sweet rhythm of her hips grinding on me almost made me come in my pants like a teenager. It was agony. The best, most pleasurable agony of my life.

I let my hands slip down from her cheeks, sliding my fingers through her riot of red hair, combing her curls with my hands, gathering the locks in my hands like a live thing, using them to angle her head so I could go deeper with my kiss. She took it all, stroked her tongue along mine just as hungrily, ground against my thigh appreciatively as she enjoyed the friction in time with my tongue thrusting in her mouth.

It felt strange, intense, like I was doing more than kissing a woman I'd gone out for drinks with. What I wanted most was to taste the scream of my name on a wave of her orgasm. I was rigid, painfully hard as we kissed. I couldn't even let myself imagine the relief of parting her thighs wide and sinking into her wet heat. I was barely holding on in the abyss of that kiss, and if I let myself fantasize even for a second, I knew I'd come. In fact, if she kept rocking against me, I might come anyway. I pulled back from her mouth, withdrew my knee from between her hot, strong thighs. She took a step toward me as I pulled away, her lips clinging to mine, her arms still around my neck. I stepped back another foot, rubbed my hands over my face. I was sure she could see the frown of concentration from reining in my desires. I was probably scowling with the effort.

"So, good night then," she grinned, pink with pleasure.

She rose up on tiptoe and pressed a quick kiss to my lips that staggered me. I reached out for the railing to hold on to. Because it wasn't just the gesture, the affection in it that got to me. It was the fiery jolt of pleasure I got from Maggie's kiss, a three-second, barely-there kiss that felt like a building just went up in flames, consumed by lashing fire, bright against a dark sky.

I nodded to her, watched her unlock the door and go inside before I drove off. I gritted my teeth all the way back to the B&B. I barely made it in the room and locked the door before I had my pants unzipped and my cock in my hand, turgid and pulsing, thick in my punishing fist. I leaned my head back against the door as I jerked off, my eyes shut on images of Maggie, her big, soft breasts a swell against my chest, her tongue in my mouth, my hands full of her hair. In my fantasy, I hitched up her knee to my hips and opened her to me. With two fingers I found her soaking wet sex, massaged her, making a slick mess of her before I drove my cock in hard, all at once in a deep thrust that lifted her off the ground as I braced her against the car and fucked her without saying a word. As I imagined her tight, slick pussy around me, I came in fierce spurts, my whole body shaken with the force of it.

It still wasn't enough. The sexual tension between us wouldn't go away. Not if I jerked off every hour until I left this little town in the dust. Nothing would satisfy me but Maggie herself, all of her naked on this bed she had made. Something about that appealed to me, letting her be the one to make those fresh clean sheets all dirty, our sex pressing her into the mattress and letting her find her release in that bed, under those blankets.

9

———

MAGGIE

I was surprised I could even walk up the porch steps. He had my legs so weak, my panties so wet from that kiss. No, it had been more than a kiss. So when I went inside and locked the door, I turned off my porch lights so no one could see what I was about to do.

I had never, ever done it before. Not like that. Not jerking my pants down, leaning my shoulder against the door and shoving my hand into my soaking wet panties. I didn't play around either. I stuffed my fingers between my wet, quivering lips while I worked my thumb over my clit hard and fast. I slithered to the floor when I came, grunting with the release. I just sat there with my pants around my knees, my fingers drenched and still crammed inside my panties while my inner muscles quivered with the aftershocks.

After a long shower, I called my sister.

"I'm a failed slut," I said.

"What? Were you really bad in bed or what?" she mumbled sleepily.

"No. We didn't' get that far. I didn't have the nerve to

do it. I can't have a fling. I'm not built that way. I'm not equipped to handle what he was giving me."

"Oh, God, is he weird? Did he whip out a ball gag?"

"Oh my god, no! He's here on business, why would he have a ball gag with him?" I said.

"So what did Company Man do?"

"He asked me to go back to his room and spend the night. I said no," I said miserably.

"Not into him?"

"Yes into him. Super into him," I shouted without meaning to.

"Jeez, woman, you woke me up to yell at me about how bad you want the guy you turned down? I'm not a therapist. Call the health department and see if they have a specialist for stupid chicks who refuse to get laid," she said grouchily.

"I'm not stupid. I barely know him. But I have no control over my body when I'm around him. When he kissed me, I thought I was going to come on the spot, I swear to God."

"You can't come from a kiss," she said dismissively.

"I would've said that too, but now that I've kissed him, or he kissed me, I should say," I sighed. "It was that good."

"Sound's great. Why'd you say no again?"

"I wish I could've gone with him. It would've been easier than this. I'm suffering. I'm just not the kind of girl who can go home with some guy. I'm sorry."

"Don't tell me you're sorry. You're the one sitting around with some girly blue balls," she laughed, "Get out your vibrator and—"

"Look, that is not going to solve anything. This is like nuclear-level sexual tension. My body responds to him in a way that I can't even explain."

"I think you're making this too complicated," Ella said. "But if you need to get to know him better first, do it."

"He's only here for a week or two. There is no way I'll know him well enough by then. And I have only slept with one guy, and that was in a serious relationship. I can't do a one-nighter or a fling. It doesn't compute with me."

"So how's that working out? Feel good? Pleased with yourself?" she teased.

"Fine. I'm miserable. I wish I could have let myself spend the night with him. I'd be curled up in his bed now with his arms around me. He has great arms. He has great everything," I said miserably.

"Okay, well that sucks for you, but I really need to get back to sleep. Night," she said and hung up, that heartless bitch. She totally went back to sleep while I was being dramatic about my girly blue balls. Because I had wanted to stay, but I had to face the fact that I'm not the kind of woman who could spend the night with a man she barely knew without regretting it later.

Regret was a bigger problem than this misery. Regret and potential heartbreak were a recipe for disaster.

So I went to sleep, went to work, and dealt with Payton's tantrums and being shorthanded because one of the aids had come down with pinkeye. Which meant we had to disinfect everything and reteach handwashing skills just in case.

I was in the middle of singing "Happy Birthday" to demonstrate how long to wash your hands with soap when Jeremiah walked into the common area of my daycare center. And took all the air with him. I stopped mid-song and looked at him. The kids tried to finish singing on their own, but being two and three-year-olds, they threw in some lyrics from Twinkle Twinkle Little Star to try and finish up in style. I laughed and started over, finishing the lesson properly and sending them to the sinks in their respective age-level rooms to do some guided practice at thorough handwashing and germ-killing.

"That was fantastic," he said, sidling over to me, looking as usual, like a model for an expensive catalog. "You guys should cut an album."

"Our mash-ups are legendary," I said. "You should have heard our Jingle Bells and Lizzo mix at the holidays. It was epic."

"It must've been. I hope you don't mind that I stopped by. I wanted to get a sense of the full economic impact this factory has on the surrounding community. Would you mind showing me around?"

"Sure. I think you got a general idea of the number of students here. We have forty-nine full-time kids ages 2-4, plus the sixteen in our accredited pre-K program for 4and 5-year olds. Our toddler room fluctuates because some of them come part-time, but at full attendance we have eleven of those as well. That's a total of seventy-eight kids divided among seven classrooms. We have a full bathroom in each room, plus changing facilities for three at once in the toddler room and trainer potties. Every room has a work sink as well for handwashing, art, and snack time. Our kitchen is separate and accessible only with a lock fob for safety reasons. We passed all health department inspections every year with no demerits."

"It sounds like a full-service facility. You must be very proud of it. How long has it been open?" he said.

He followed me into the kitchen and looked over the place. When I went out ahead of him, his hand brushed the small of my back. It was electric, scorching arousal whisking up my spine.

"I opened three years ago, right after I graduated college"

"That's impressive," he said.

I reached out and brushed a nonexistent piece of lint off his shoulder just to touch him, to see the muscle in his jaw tighten at my touch. I liked seeing how he was just as affected as I was.

"I knew there was a need in the market," I said. "And it's been very satisfying making a success of it. The first year was basically figuring out what worked—what to have for meals that the kids would eat but was still nutritious enough to meet state guidelines and how big the portion sizes should be, what do we ask parents to send versus what do we stock as supplies, that sort of thing. It was a lot of trial and error. About halfway through year two, I added the toddler room at parent request, which meant hiring more personnel and figuring out tuition rates for younger, more care-intensive kids."

"It sounds like you've had quite a journey," he said as I showed him the last classroom on the tour.

"The babies are napping. I wouldn't open that door for anything, but you can see through the window there," I said.

"Will you go out with me?" he said suddenly.

"What?"

"Dinner tonight. Whatever time you name. We can go someplace in the next town. I don't want people here being mad at you because of me. But I'm not considerate enough to just leave you alone. I still want to have dinner with you."

"I'd like that," I said, though I knew I probably shouldn't.

10

JEREMIAH

I picked her up at her house. A silky skirt swirled around her knees as she got in my car. She had on red lipstick I wanted to kiss right off, smearing it over both of our faces.

"You look lovely," I said.

"Thank you," she said almost demurely.

"I want to clear the air here. It's bothered me since we went for a drink and I propositioned you. I'm concerned that I insulted you. I meant no offense," I said diffidently.

"You didn't. I just couldn't take you up on it. So the situation itself was uncomfortable."

"I apologize," I said.

"Please don't. It's fine," she said.

I saw her relax a little, and I reached for her hand and held it.

"I don't know what the hell I'm doing with you, if that helps," I said.

"It does," she looked at me gravely, not joking.

"Good. Does that make two of us?"

"It does," she said again.

"Then I'll confess something else. Part of the reason I'm

taking you out of town for dinner is because I don't want you to have to be seen consorting with the enemy by the pro-factory people in town. The other reason is that I want privacy for us. I don't want to run into your friends and relatives. I'm sure they're nice people, but they're not invited."

"Oh really. Our conversation won't be suitable for my grandma then?"

"Definitely not," I said.

"Tell me more."

"I can't get you off my mind," I said, not even meaning to. She was in my rental car again, smelling of vanilla and that scent was like truth serum to me or something.

"It's complicated," she said.

"It is. I'm your enemy, here to be the Grinch that stole the economy or whatever. We shouldn't even know each other's names. You should be a nameless annoyed citizen to me. Not Maggie with the great laugh who built a successful business on her own, and who lives in an adorable house with two chimneys and has at least four different colors of Chucks to wear to work, and who makes a killer potato casserole. You're remarkable. I couldn't ignore you even if my body would let me. You have to know by now that I want you."

"I suspected," she said teasingly, "just as I'm sure you suspected that I want you."

"So we agree there's an attraction, a stronger than normal attraction here. The chemistry is scorching. But we're not going to act on it. It's too complicated, plus I'm only in town for a couple of weeks. As an afterthought, we're mortal enemies facing off over the fate of an underper-forming local chicken processing plant. So that's three strikes against us."

"I think that's two. Because 'it's complicated' includes the mortal enemies thing."

"Only two strikes? So we should go for it?" I joked.

"Hardly. But we can still get to know each other, spend time together, torture ourselves. And touch each other unnecessarily a whole lot."

"That's a clearer plan than most people have in a long-term relationship."

"Yep. I'm Cosmo-ready. I had the DTR."

"What?"

"The talk where we Define the Relationship. We laid out our expectations. We both know we're in this to yearn with nearly intolerable lust for a few dates before you leave."

"And we're not sleeping together."

"Exactly."

"This is the strangest relationship ever."

"That's because it isn't one. We just enjoy each other's company too much to stay away, even though we're both frustrated about it."

"That's true," I said as I pulled into a parking place. "We have a reservation."

"I've never been here. My parents came here on their twenty-fifth anniversary a few years ago. It's really fancy," she said.

"Glad I could impress you," I said wryly.

Then I went around and opened her door. As she stepped out, she walked right into my arms.

"When we defined the relationship, you said there'd be unnecessary touching," I said lightly, taking her in my arms, "but you didn't mention the necessary kissing."

"I have on red lipstick. It's supposed to keep us from kissing," she protested.

"It's a failure then," I said, my mouth covering hers.

Her hair spilled into my hand as I palmed her head, nipped at her lips and then parted them, kissing her so intensely that I felt a shudder rip through my body when her tongue touched mine. It was a searing shiver of yes and now and more as I took her mouth, claimed her with every stroke of my tongue. She clung to my back so hard that I could almost feel her nails digging into my bare skin the way they would if I had her on her back on my bed, driving my rigid cock into her. She bit my lip, grazing it with her tongue, and I made a sound in the back of my throat that was almost a growl. It was all I could do not to drag her into the backseat of that car like a caveman.

She was the one to pull away. I would have found the strength to break the kiss, but I was grateful she'd mustered the resolve first. I stepped back, breathing heavily.

"You have my lipstick all over your face," she said, reaching her hand out and touching my lips.

"It's all over you, too. We could always skip dinner and go have a shower back at my room."

"See, you can't say stuff like that. I'll get the wrong idea."

"That's giving you the right idea. The idea that I want to take you to bed and keep you there for the next four days at least."

"Four days?"

"Is that too long?"

"I've never been involved in anything that took more than fifteen minutes," she laughed.

"I could change that. It would be an honor to set that right," I said, too serious all at once. Fifteen minutes? Did the men in this backwater know nothing about the female body? It was a matter of pride to remedy the deficiency she'd suffered.

"Let me," I said, my voice more urgent than I meant it to be, if I'd even meant to say it at all.

She touched my lips with her fingertips again, she reached into her purse with the other hand and took out some packet she opened. For a second I thought it was a condom, but she pulled out a moist towelette and cleaned the lipstick off my face. When she handed it to me so I could return the favor, it was smeared with streaks of red. I carefully wiped off the smudges of lipstick around her mouth, on her chin. Once I'd cleaned her up, I kissed her again. And again. Right there in front of the restaurant. Our arms were around each other when a man cleared his throat.

"Pardon me, are you Leeds, the seven o'clock reservation, party of two?" the voice said.

I lifted my mouth from hers reluctantly.

"Yes," I ground out without turning around.

"We can offer you a private table for the evening. Upstairs in the VIP room."

"Very good," I said, my eyes never leaving Maggie's.

"Are you sure?" she whispered.

"Sounds perfect to me," I murmured, offering her my arm. She took it and we went into the restaurant with our heads held high. Up a curving flight of stairs tucked back in a corner, we found ourselves in a round, velvet booth in a small, low-ceilinged room lit by candles. I had preordered the chef's tasting menus and the wine, so the waiter had no reason to bother us.

"I appreciate discreet service," I said.

"If you wish it, we can use the dumbwaiter," the maître'd indicated a small door in the wall.

"That sounds great," I said.

Just like that, we had the plush, dim room all to ourselves. There was absolutely no way we'd make it out of this dinner without fucking no matter what our best intentions had been when we defined the brief and celibate relationship we'd discussed. She glanced at me. Her eyes were wide and bright, and I could tell she was nervous.

"I'm not going to do anything you don't want me to do," I said, "that's also a matter of pride."

"We should have waiters come up here and refill our water glasses and stuff to keep us honest," she said.

"If you're uncomfortable we can change to a table downstairs," I offered.

"That isn't what I want. I want to be here with you. I'm just not confident that I can keep from, you know..."

"I'm a strong-willed man. If you truly don't want to have sex with me, I can assure you we won't, even if you beg, which I'm perfectly capable of making you do," I said archly.

"I don't doubt that," she said, her voice shaky, "but I don't expect you to be responsible for keeping me from doing something I'd regret. That's on me."

"So what are you saying?"

"I'm saying if you make me beg, give me what I'm begging for."

My mouth watered when she said it. I wanted to give her a screaming orgasm right that second. But I knew what she meant. She meant that she'd take responsibility for her own actions like any grown-ass adult. She didn't mean she wanted me to take her in a restaurant booth. So it would be an exercise in restraint. I could handle that. I nodded.

The light above the dumbwaiter flashed on, and I removed a tray of glasses and the wine as well as an antipasto platter. We picked at that and gazed, literally gazed at each other. There was such pleasure in just looking at her in knowing that we shared the same ridiculously impure thoughts about each other. That we were, by mutual agreement, not entertaining those thoughts. It was rather like we were partners in crime.

It was dangerous to forget we were adversaries, that no matter how close she curled up to me in the booth, in daylight we were on opposite sides of a life-changing decision. My employer needed me to assess the viability of keeping this plant open versus relocating overseas for a cheaper alternative. Maggie's friends and community and daycare business all depended on keeping the factory operational and open. We were at cross-purposes. There was no way we could ever make anything work between us, not even in a short-term fling. Which she wasn't willing to have anyway.

So why was I wasting a free evening and hundreds of dollars on dinner with a woman who would never go to bed with me? Simple. I liked her. I wanted to spend time with her. In fact, there was nothing I'd rather be doing than hearing about her students and talking with her about my life. She was brash and funny and direct, and I liked her.

Halfway through our appetizers, I found myself telling her more about my childhood.

"I was the one who bought cheap bulk rubber bands, the colored ones, and sold them at a profit to little kids who used them to make bracelets. I was all about generating money, and my brother was the protective one, the athletic one. I was good with numbers, started tutoring for ten bucks a half hour when I was in fifth grade. I knew how to turn my skills into cash. I was covering the water bill before I was thirteen and swung new shoes for my brother and me for Christmas by that time as well. While my brother was trying to score an athletic scholarship that never came through—hence his enlistment—I got my tuition paid at a state college and still tutored did work-study for my books and housing. My mom still thinks to this day that the scholarship covered my housing and everything. I was resourceful, but my brother was out there saving lives."

"He sounds like a great guy. I have two older sisters, so I know about being competitive at home. One of my favorite memories is making and decorating Christmas cookies with my sisters every year. My mom always took us to the nursing home to deliver the cookies, too. What was your favorite memory?"

"My mom always read to us. Even when she was dead tired from working two jobs, she'd stay up to read us a library book. That's where I got the idea how important education was, and how much more there was to her than just some woman whose life got derailed by a pregnancy. She was really into the Harry Potter books. We read all the books, watched all the movies on TV. I remember us saving up to get her a bathrobe, this stupid bathrobe that looked like a Hogwarts student robe. She loved it. To this day, she has it on a hook in her bathroom. Thank God it's a nicer bathroom than she used to have. That was my number one, taking a corporate job instead of starting my own firm. Hadley paid me enough as a hiring bonus to make a down payment on a house for her."

"You bought her a house?"

"When I was twenty-four. I paid it off a year later. I retired my mom. That was my goal."

"That's so sweet."

"Nothing I do could ever repay her for the sacrifices she

made or the shit she put up with raising us. My brother was genius at forging her name."

"Why would you forge her name?"

"To get free breakfast and lunch at school. We qualified but she had this thing about not taking charity, paying her own way. So we just signed up for ourselves in third grade, saved her a fortune on feeding growing boys. If she ever noticed that those boxes of cereal lasted a long time, she never said," I shook my head. "Now that I think about it, I'm positive she knew. I mean she was on top of stuff, and she's a smart woman. But we thought we were so clever, she probably let us think we had her fooled."

Maggie wrapped her arms around me and kissed my cheek, "That's very sweet. Every woman deserves such a son, so protective and resourceful."

"Thank you. I've been working my whole life to make her proud. I'm not sure she'd be proud of the job I'm doing now, shutting down businesses that support a whole town," I shook my head ruefully.

"She's proud that you're a hard worker, and you're not as much of a bastard as you pretend to be."

I gave a wry laugh, "There's a compliment for you."

"You have a heart, even if you do try and hide it."

"Okay, so I've never actually told anyone all of that. So tell me something you've never told anyone."

"What, you showed me yours so I have to show you mine?" she laughed.

"Exactly. That's the date. I'm buying dinner so I demand an emotional confession."

"Most guys just expect me to put out. They also end up disappointed."

"No deep, dark secrets?"

"Maybe a few. Okay, you know Payton, the kid with the

massive tantrums? I have to rotate two of my teachers in that room. I've told all the parents it's due to a licensing requirement, but it's really because it's so stressful dealing with him all day that no one can take it full time. I do my rotation in that room when I have to sub. I'll move the teacher out of that room into the room with an absentee staff and I'll take over. His behaviors are super exhausting. We love him to bits, and he's a great kid, but it's a lot. So I fake-splained a staffing decision to keep from hurting his parents' feelings. There, that's a confession."

"Is this the one that loves Legos?"

"Yeah, you remember that?" she said.

"And he has to play with like the big fat blocks instead because it's a choking hazard otherwise. Yeah, I listen," I grinned, "So what if we got some of those big magnet triangle blocks?"

"The tiny magnets imbedded in them are a choking hazard and they can cause intestinal damage," she said.

"Wow. You know a lot about how dangerous everything is."

"Yes. Part of the job, but it's sweet that you thought of it."

"Tinker toys? I loved those as a kid, we used to check them out of the library. No small pieces."

"Aren't they wood? Splinters."

"I'm sure we can find plastic ones," I assured her. "Leave it to me. I think if your daycare received a donation of some Tinker toys, his behavior might improve. Especially if he has to earn the right to play with them."

"You're kind of an evil genius, Company Man," she smiled.

She kissed my cheek. It was a terrific feeling, one I hadn't had in ages. Because I had just come up with a constructive way to solve a problem instead of just doing inspections and shutting places down. I liked her affection and her gratitude, but I also liked taking an interest in her kids and their problems.

"Anything deeper and darker?" I ventured.

"Okay, I've only slept with one guy."

I tried not to look taken aback. I couldn't fathom why a woman so beautiful would have only had one partner. "Oh," was all I could say.

She looked away for a brief moment before turning her gaze back to me. "Not exactly worldly, am I?" she joked.

"You're perfect," I replied.

"I've only slept with one guy."

I leaned forward and kissed the place just where her neck met her shoulder. I felt the ripple of tension shudder through her, felt the answering sizzle of arousal in my own body. Just touching her, tasting her skin was like a drug to me. My mouth slid to her collarbone, her hand in my hair. My hand grazed her breast, that tight nipple hard against the brush of my hungry fingers. I lifted my head, cleared my throat.

She was trembling. I had made her tremble, and it felt so good to know I could make her feel that way. I couldn't stop myself from grinning.

"I think our food is here," she said, scooting a little away from me in the booth and indicating the flashing light over the dumbwaiter. "Also that smile makes you look arrogant."

"What man wouldn't be arrogant if he could make you tremble?" I said, my voice sounding huskier than it should.

I expected her to laugh, but she looked at me dead in the eyes and said, "You're the only man who ever has."

I felt that down to my bones. I gritted my teeth just to steel myself to go get our food. I hated our food and the entire restaurant right then, because I wanted to lay her back in that plush velvet booth and bury my face between her legs until she was crying out in ecstasy, her legs jerking around over my shoulders with her orgasm. I carried the tray from the dumbwaiter with all the grace of a rhino in a hurry. I thunked it down on the table, making the candle flames shiver with the impact. She laughed.

"Maybe don't quit your day job to become a waiter," she said as she took the bowls of steaming lobster bisque from beneath the silver domed lid.

"It wasn't my ambition anyway."

"And what's your ambition?" she asked, just a hint of naughtiness in her voice.

"I don't think you want me to answer that. I think you want to eat your soup in silence," I said, my teeth still gritted. She laughed airily.

"Something funny?" I asked, my voice dangerous as I trailed the backs of my fingers up her arm. She jerked at my touch like she'd grabbed a live wire.

"It just makes me so happy that it's hard for you, too," she said. "That I'm sitting here nervous as a cat because I'm half-afraid I'll launch myself into your lap and you're having as hard of a time with it as I am."

I leaned in, my lips brushing her ear, "Oh it's definitely hard. I want to taste you right now, and when I shut my eyes to try and sleep all I imagine is being between your thighs."

She gave the softest moan, like agony, and then I saw her bite down hard on her full lower lip.

"Did that make you wet? Did it make you want me more?" I said shamelessly against her ear, barely above a whisper.

"Yes," she said, nodding almost frantically. "I feel like I've gone crazy. I can't think when I'm around you. All I do is feel and want and then you say something like that—you're going to push me over the edge. I don't want to do something I'll regret. I'm shaking, Jeremiah."

"I want to make you tremble like that, want to make you shake so hard all you can do is cling to me and beg."

"Then what would you do?" she whispered.

"Then I'd give you whatever you were begging me for. I wouldn't make you wait. I couldn't. Because I'd give you anything you asked me for right now, just to kiss you, I think."

It felt like a fever dream, too bright, too intense. *Please don't ask me to save the factory. Please don't be playing me to get what you want from Hadley Corp,* I thought, wondering how long it had been since I wished so hard for something.

"Then kiss me," she said.

All that was left of her bright lipstick had to smear all over our faces then, because I had to have her mouth. Partly in relief that she hadn't been winding me up into horny desperation just to try and manipulate me into saving the plant, and partly because I was in fact in a state of urgent, aroused desperation. The lush kiss of her soft lips on mine stole my breath. I was in control of the kiss, mastering her, stroking my tongue into her mouth just the way I wanted to. I reminded myself of that so I wasn't completely swept away on a tide of sensation. Passion welled up in me, my whole body rigid with need. I kissed her, devoured her without holding back.

For a few minutes there I would've sworn I was insane, driven by nothing but the crackling sexual tension between us, the firestorm of passion. Then I got control of myself and backed away. I even took a drink of wine, as if that would help. A bucket of ice water over my head wouldn't help. I got up and paced around the small, opulent room that seemed designed for romance, for lushness and kisses in the shadows. I stalked back and forth a few times to put distance between us. She was trying bravely to eat the soup we'd let go cold. She patted her lips with a napkin, those sensuous, rosy lips that were flushed from being kissed. I nearly groaned from watching her use a damn napkin.

I loaded the bowls back on the tray and shoved it into the dumbwaiter irritably. This had been a mistake. I liked her too well, and we were way too attracted to each other. We couldn't afford to be alone this way if we meant to avoid full-on sex. I rubbed a hand over my eyes and tried to focus on other things. The six thousand dollars I won on the Super Bowl last winter. The Hermes tie I found in a vintage shop in Charlotte for seventeen dollars. The pool I had put in behind my mom's house so she could relax and swim whenever she wanted. Those were good things to think about, nice, wholesome, nonsexual things that might get us through the fish course if her leg didn't brush up against mine.

She made me feel the way the Sports Illustrated Swimsuit issue made me feel when I was fifteen. Like the entire world was a thirst trap and my constant arousal was obvious. Like the only thought my brain was able to produce was a completely X-rated request. I sat down and drained my water glass.

"You okay there, Company Man?" she said archly, a self-satisfied grin on her face.

"Now who's arrogant?"

"Me? What do I have to be arrogant about? Except you offering me everything up to half your kingdom or whatever just to kiss me."

"I was carried away."

"I was there for that kiss. It was in no way an overreaction. I thought briefly of buying new sheets for your hotel room, because we were going to mess those up. They'd be filthy."

"God, don't say filthy. Or anything else. Everything sounds so wrong right now."

"Wrong?"

"Dirty," I corrected grimly.

"Is that a bad thing? A wrong thing?'

"Only if you're serious about not sleeping together."

"I'm serious. I'm not trying to be a tease."

"You're not. You've been very honest with me from the beginning. That doesn't stop me from getting ideas," I said.

"I think dinner's ready. The light's flashing again. I'll go get it this time."

"A gentleman doesn't make a lady fetch her own dinner. And we're pretending I'm a gentleman, right?" I said and slid out of the booth to retrieve the tray.

"Does a gentleman reserve a private room and forbid the staff to enter?" she said wickedly.

"Probably not. I also don't drive a pair of horses hitched to a buggy or have a valet lay out my clothes," I said. "So we've agreed I'm just impersonating a gentleman. Your dinner, my lady."

I lifted the lid to reveal a sumptuous looking fish course with a light sauce. We both dug in and ate for a few minutes, as if by mutual agreement to have dinner instead of just making out and then talking about how we wanted to sleep together but we wouldn't. The fish was excellent, the wine was better, and she never failed to make me laugh and like her better every time she spoke.

By the time I was feeding her lobster dunked in drawn butter and she was licking the butter off my fingers, we decided it was time to cut the evening short. No dessert for us, because it was getting too intense. The second she sucked the tip of my finger into her mouth, I went rock hard and pulled back only by sheer force of will.

"I think we should call it a night," I said, my voice thick with reluctance and arousal.

She nodded like her head was on a spring, her eyes feverish, her hand reaching out toward me even as I stepped back, shoving my hands into the pockets of my pants that were now uncomfortably tight. I spoke to the manager, paid the bill, and she brought us a pair of desserts in to-go boxes. II wanted to do nothing more than throw down the boxes, back Maggie up against the pillar right there in the restaurant and jerk her panties down, bury my throbbing cock inside her and let her ride me until we both collapsed from exhaustion and the kind of orgasm that could kill a man. I took out a handkerchief and blotted sweat off my forehead. I was well and truly overheated.

I drove her back to her house, the silence thick with frustrated desire and nothing to say to relieve it. We were still enemies. She wasn't the sort of woman willing to have a week or two of steamy hate-sex, and I liked her too well for my own good already. When I pulled up in front of her adorable house, she turned to me.

"I had a really nice time this evening. I mean, it was wild and miserable, but nice," she said.

I reached for her without a word. The sharp ache of desire made me ruthless, unable to speak. I took her face in my hands and feasted on her moth, devouring her lips, her tongue, making her pant and cling to me and do everything just the way I wanted it. She had a natural talent for driving me wild, it seemed.

Trailing fingertips down her neck, I ran my hand down her chest, making her tremble again and arch into my palm as my hand found her aching, eager breast, so full and heavy in my hand. I groaned into her mouth as I felt it, the weight and longing, the needy ache of it, and the way the tip responded to the slightest brush of my thumb. I felt her tighten, going hard and tight under my touch. She needed it just like I did, I thought.

I worked her nipple a little harder as I kissed her, my thumb keeping pace with the onslaught of my relentless tongue, my determination to taste her as much as possible. She seemed willing to let me, seemed like she was so turned on that she'd probably let me do practically anything at that point. I wanted to pull her under me, to come down over her in the car, shove my knee between her thighs and work her hard until she gave me everything I needed, hot, tight, and deep.

We kissed for so long I wasn't sure I knew how to do anything else. This was my job and my life now, sitting in a rental car making out with Maggie. I was okay with that.

With a ragged breath that was almost a sob, she pulled back from me and took my hands in hers, squeezing my fingers tightly. Her breathing was fast and heavy, and so was mine.

"Thank you for dinner," she said, her voice a little shaky.

"You're welcome. That kiss was—"

"I know what it was. It was a sign that I should say good night, go in the house alone and lock the door."

"I'm not going to break down your door," I said, as if I hadn't thought of doing just that.

"I know. It's to remind me that I shouldn't run back out and chase your car," she laughed. It was a big, hearty, self-deprecating laugh that made me feel warm and good all the way through.

"Damn it all, Maggie," I burst out, "this is impossible. There's no reason in the world we should even be on speaking terms, much less kissing each other's clothes off in a parked car. It's ridiculous. I'm not sure we'll survive it."

"There's no way it would work. Not even in the short term. So let's agree that the entire attraction is a stupid freak of nature, something to do with hormones or barometric pressure, I don't know," she said, "and be nodding acquaintances from here on out. I'll say good morning if I see you. But I won't kiss you again."

"That's a solid plan. Except, I wish you'd told me that before our last kiss."

"You couldn't have made it any better, trust me," she said with that shaky edge back in her voice that made my heart rate spike in response.

"It would have been different. I would have approached it differently."

"Be careful, that sounds almost—sensitive," she said, trying to joke.

"I want a do-over. A last kiss when I know it's the one. The only kiss I'll ever get to give you," I said. My heart pounded. I felt an urgency, a blinding need to do this, to kiss her once and for all, to let my mouth, my body tell her everything I couldn't say.

She nodded, "Okay. That's fair."

I felt a flood of relief. I hadn't expected her to agree. I'd thought I'd have to persuade her, to demand it. So the unfamiliar sensation of gratitude filled me for an instant. Then I flexed my hands, took in a long breath.

"Do you have to prepare yourself?" she said, teasing.

"Maybe. This is going to be the kiss you compare every other kiss to for the rest of your life. So I think we should both be sure we're ready," I said, dead serious, seeing the humor in her eyes drain away and become a dark glitter.

I brushed her hair back from her face, taking a moment to memorize the wild, silky mass of her curls as they wrapped around my questing fingers.

I brushed a kiss on her cheek soft as a shadow. She tried to turn her head, press her lips to mine.

"Don't rush me," I almost growled.

Nuzzling her ear, the spot just below it, and I felt her arms around me, her hands on my back. I knew she wouldn't sit there passively, but the pressure of her arms, the clutching of her hands was a powerful sensation. I parted my lips, gave a slow suck on her throat just beneath her ear. Her body bowed to mine in response, fingers digging in on my back from the shock of that.

I kissed her jaw, her chin, making my way to her lips slowly, making her moan a couple of times, even though my hands hadn't moved south of her hair yet. She was supple and responsive, arching against me, parting her kiss-reddened lips and wanting it from me. It was so hard to keep myself leashed, to go slowly and savor this.

I could have her right now, could take her in the front seat of this car and she'd beg for more. She'd never object. I could spend myself inside of her, sate us both and never have to apologize. She was as hungry, as needy as I was. She would regret it, probably weep over it later. Why did I care about that? I could have what I wanted, what I had a primal drive to finish. It was in my power to take her now, and she'd thank me for it in the moment, feel sorry later, perhaps a little betrayed or taken advantage of. That shouldn't bother me. Why couldn't I overlook that? Why couldn't I just charge ahead and make her mine?

Instead, I did exactly what I'd promised her. I gave her a

goodbye kiss to burn down the record books for greatest kisses of all time. If there was such a record book, this would have turned the book to ashes with its passion and fire.

My mouth rocked over hers, locking our lips, clinging, frantic and wistful and achingly slow at the same time.

I wish I could give you more than this, my mouth told her without a word.

Her lips parted, her tongue darted out to touch mine.

My tongue slid inside her mouth, gentle and questing.

I cradled her head in my hands, tender, cherishing, treasuring her in a way I had never imagined holding any woman. The woman I'd wanted to take hard and fast in the front seat of a car, just to get inside her, just to pound her until I came—I was holding her like she was made of porcelain, like she was the most essential thing in the world to me. I could no longer imagine having her anyplace but a bed, an old-fashioned, four poster bed with that red hair fanned out on the pillow as I worshiped every curve of that body.

I kept kissing her, sensual and tender, rocking my tongue into her mouth, in and out, nipping her lips, sipping at them, then going deep with my tongue and making her shake in my hands. I gave her every longing I had, every fantasy I'd had of her, every way I wanted to make love to her, every idea I'd had during that dinner. Kissing her was another place, another planet. Eventually I had to stop, to press her into my arms, kiss her tumbled hair. My heart pounded like I'd run a marathon or climbed a mountain. Which I had. I had kissed her without making love to her.

I pressed her into my chest, let her cling to me, hold on to me for a moment until we could both recover. When she lifted her head, her eyes were bright as if with tears. She leaned up and pressed her lips to mine, our lips clinging to each other, a soft, sweet kiss. Then I got out of the car, opened her door.

I did something I had never done before. I took her hand and lifted it to my lips. I kissed her hand. I said good night, a single, final caress to her cheek with the backs of my fingers. Then I turned and watched her walk inside.

I drove back to the B&B and stayed up doing emails and reading reports, because there was no way I could sleep. I missed her. I might not see her again. I had agreed not to seek her out, agreed it was a bad idea. We were enemies. This was going nowhere.

I thought of her while I worked. I thought of her while I was at the gym doing punishing interval training just to try and work the tension out of my body. She consumed me, even at a distance.

11

MAGGIE

I had to do something besides lie awake thinking of that kiss. I felt completely exposed, completely cherished. I felt oversexed from a single kiss. Like I had what my friend Cat called dick withdrawal, like I wanted it all the time, like I was deprived of a drug I needed to function. To call him a thirst trap was an understatement. I wanted him with every breath. I was in danger of wearing out a vibrator on fantasies about his hands in my hair. Just thinking about the way he'd kissed me below my ear, the sudden hard suck that had shot shock waves straight to my clit, had me ready to go off in an instant.

I even messaged Layla and asked for her recommendations. Layla was the local sex toy connoisseur, who frequently told us at margarita nights that there was one for every occasion.

"What do you use when completely frustrated?"

"Internal or suction?" she asked, as if I knew the difference.

"Idk," I answered.

"Suction will curl your toes first, internal like a rabbit or a dildo if you want to pound."

"The pounding," I said, "Definitely."

She messaged me links, told me the best ones. I ordered one. I paid for overnight shipping. It wouldn't be what I needed, but it might take the edge off. And if something didn't take the edge off soon, I was going to end up in a mental institution. I was crabby, irritable, my mom even asked if I had bad PMS this month or what because I cut her off when she was telling a story about someone from church, and I had already heard it. I was usually way more patient.

When the toy came, I gave it a workout, but it was nothing, nothing like the way I'd felt with Jeremiah Leeds's hand in my hair and his mouth on mine. It was a pale imitation, a machine to do a man's job. I almost cried with frustration over the slight flutters of insufficient orgasm that it produced. In frustration, I scrubbed my kitchen and tried to make soup.

I threw myself into work. I needed a program to encourage the community and increase interest in my business. An after-school program with homework help and fun activities would help the non-factory parents who had different shift dismissal times, and it would add in some school-age kids of current clients. That's increased support for the factory workers and adding enrichment for the kids. I started looking up easy STEM activities for them, planned to run the program myself with one aid, possibly even hiring a high school helper for assistance with snack and homework. There were plenty of kids at the school who were doing family consumer sciences classes and could use the money. I made myself a list and got started. My staff was receptive to it and we worked up a serious plan. In no time I had a flier to post at the factory as well as a copy up on our Facebook and website.

I decided to take the fliers up myself. I mean, sure, a parent at drop-off would've happily taken the stack of red paper up to the factory and had them posted around, but this was something I should see to myself. For proper placement and maximum exposure. And in NO WAY was I trying to run into Jeremiah Leeds.

I stood around chatting with Lindsay, a girl I graduated with who was now the assistant to the foreman.

"Sure thing, I'll post these up everywhere. You know how much we love the Fun Factory around here. If it wasn't for you, there's no telling how most of our line workers could make it here on time, what with your early drop-off time."

"Thanks, Lindsay. And you know how important the plant is to my daycare center, too. If it wasn't for y'all, I wouldn't have a business."

"That's right. We all work together around here to make things go right. I just wish this corporate guy would go back where he came from," she said.

"Or that he'd never come," I said grimly, although I couldn't really wish it.

"He's always around. It's all I can do to smile and say good morning like my mama taught me," Lindsay said with a huff.

"I know it's hard with all our jobs on the line," I said to her, "You coming to the game tomorrow? We could use you to cheer."

"You bet I am. I'm calling it self-care. It'll cheer me up to talk some trash at that other team. Those wimps over at the fish stick plant won't know what hit them."

"Great, I'll see you there," I said.

I loved going to cheer at the softball games. Sarah Jo sometimes came, and Layla and Lindsay were always there to holler with me. We weren't official cheerleaders and we sure as hell didn't do cartwheels, but we could pump up our players and intimidate the visiting team like nobody else. I'd have to be sure my team shirt was clean tonight.

I went up to the staff lounge on the top floor to post some more fliers. On the way up, I ran into Jeremiah. He had on a hardhat. That man had no right to look that hot in a hardhat. Not when he was here to shut down our plant and bring our town to its knees. Bastard. Sexy bastard who had his tongue in my mouth a couple nights ago. Fuck.

"Good morning, Maggie," he said. "How are you?"

"I'm good. New program down at the Fun Factory, I'm just here putting up fliers," I said brightly.

"Fun Factory?" he said. "Oh. You named your daycare after the factory. That's clever." He didn't sound like he thought it was clever at all.

"Yeah, you know how we all depend on each other in a small community, we're in this together," I said, malice in my voice.

"I know it's important to you."

"Then fix this. So we don't all lose our jobs. You can do that, right? You have the authority to decide this."

"No, I'm here to evaluate things and make a recommendation in my report."

"Then do that. Say how impressed you are with the facility and the workers and the whole community, and how we're exactly the kind of people you want consumers to think of when they see the Hadley name," I said.

"You're very persuasive," he said, "but I have to make an accurate report and submit it for the good of the corporation. Not a heartwarming sound bite. You're asking me to lie for you."

"I'm asking you to tell the truth. The workers here are dedicated, and the manager treats everybody like an important member of the team. Tomorrow's the first softball game of the season. You should come see it. It's the factory team, of course. Same factory that sponsors the Little League teams around here and does the biggest float in the homecoming parade. It's the heart of our town, Jeremiah," I said, impassioned, my face flushed.

"I see," he said, nodding, his expression grim, but his eyes flashing heat at me.

"You come to that game tomorrow at one and see if the spirit moves you. You see what this place means to us as a community. Eat a snow cone, cheer with us. Decide what's really important—this town or your boss's bottom line," I challenged.

"You're on. Where and when?"

"It's at one, out at the high school baseball field. I'd tell you how to get there, but I hear city boys just use their GPS," I said.

It was a cheap shot, but I felt resentful. Because I wanted him so much. Because I was furious at the threat to everything I held dear, and more furious that the threat came in the form of Jeremiah Leeds, the hottest man ever to put his hands on me. And I wanted his hands on me now. I couldn't help it. I could scatter those red papers on the floor and drag him into the supply closet down the hall. We could do it right up against the wall, or he could have me bent over the sink, watching me in the mirror the whole time. I felt almost sick with want.

He stood there looking so cool, so at ease with himself,

the hardhat that should have looked stupid on him looking incredible instead.

"What are you thinking? You have the craziest look in your eyes right now."

"That you don't have any right to look that hot in a hardhat," I grumbled irritably.

He laughed, "Thank you."

"Maybe when you've shut down all the factories you can go model safety gear for a catalog."

"If I shut down all the factories, no one would need the safety gear. So I doubt I'd get hired to model it," he said, smirking, "And I can tell what you're thinking now. 'That I'm an asshole.'"

"You got it in one," I said with an eye roll.

"Can you tell what I'm thinking?"

"That I'm never going to win this, that your corporate integrity or your blood oath to profit will guarantee a shutdown. That I'm a fool to even try."

"That with your face flushed like that I want to kiss you more than I've ever wanted anything. That I want to—there's a supply closet in this hall—God, I'm sorry, Maggie. I shouldn't talk like that, shouldn't admit to thinking like that. You've got me all riled up."

"Did you say riled up?" I giggled.

"Yeah, why?"

"I think we're getting to you after all if you say riled. There may be hope for you yet, Company Man. And as for what you should be sorry for, it's not thinking like that. It's being the enemy so you can't follow through. Because I know exactly where that supply closet is at and what I'd like to do there."

"Get cleaning supplies?"

"And proper safety gloves obviously," I said, "I can't

imagine you thought I would consider anything else. I'm sure there are safety regulations about what can be kept in those closets, and how many people can be in them at once."

"Two," he said. "Limit of two."

"So if we were both in there, I wouldn't be a safety violation?" I teased.

"There would be violation going on, but it wouldn't involve safety regulations. It would be you bent over that sink, meeting my eyes in the cloudy mirror above it."

I wanted to die when he said that, because it was exactly what I'd imagined.

"We had our last kiss. We agreed to part as enemies," I said almost sadly.

"Who said anything about kissing?" he said, his voice rough.

I tried to swallow, but my mouth had gone completely dry. I looked around, trying to ground myself, make myself think sensibly. My gaze settled on the camera in the ceiling. Somewhere in the building someone was monitoring all the halls and work areas for safety reasons. There was no way in hell I was going to be caught on camera going into a supply closet with the enemy. That was my concern in the moment, not breaking my vow not to get involved with him, but that I'd be caught, that people would know that I was sleeping with the enemy, or at least fucking him in closets. I couldn't let that happen. I stepped back. He stepped toward me.

"Camera," I said stupidly.

"It's not set on record. If no one is watching that screen at this second, they'd never know a thing," he said, and it was so tempting I should've gone straight to church. I shook my head.

"I'll see you at softball. You're going down, Leeds, just like the visiting team. We're going to win you over. You're going to like this town and this factory too much to destroy them. I'll see to it."

"If I wasn't working for Hadley. If I was just passing through, staying at your parents' inn, would it change anything" he asked.

I knew what he wanted me to say. He wanted me to tell him that if he weren't my enemy, I'd go to bed with him in a heartbeat, that if all that stood between us was the fact that I didn't do flings or one-night stands, then I'd break that rule and stretch out across the linen sheets of that four poster bed and let him do anything he wanted to me. But I could not say that to him. Admitting it would be shameful, and there was no point encouraging him even a little. Things weren't different. Things were the same as ever, with all the odds staked against us.

"If you were just passing through? You'd never come visit a place like this. Who are you kidding?" I said, a little harshly to avoid answering the real question.

"Why not? It's beautiful here, the people are friendly, the inn itself is lovely. I'd come here for a long weekend. If I had, would you have said yes to me?"

"If you were only some stranger and you came to the inn for check-in and I was behind the desk. No reservation?"

"No. A walk in, a stranger looking for a room for the night," he said. I warmed to the fantasy. In my mind I worked behind the counter alone, and he came in, looking tired, looking rumpled and handsome as hell.

"What would you do?"

"I'd ask if you wanted coffee or something strong," I said, a little breathless.

"What if I said all I wanted was you, the beautiful girl behind the counter?"

"I'd say I wasn't on the menu. That you had a long trip and needed some rest."

"What if I didn't rest alone? What if you came to show me to my room?"

I stepped back, "You're welcome to attend the softball game tomorrow. But that's all. We agreed."

"I'll see you there," he said with a smile.

I turned on my heel and went back downstairs without posting the rest of my fliers. For the first time I felt nervous about a softball game. Nervous about what he'd think of our small-town amusements and about whether I was going to be able to keep my panties on and still win this war.

12

JEREMIAH

Going to a local softball game to see the factory team play the first match-up of the season was not on my carefully formulated list of things to do while I was assessing the viability of the plant. But nothing would keep me from going just to see Maggie. She was irresistible all the time, but when she was fired up over something she believed in, like keeping this factory open, she was even more delectable.

Did I feel conflicted? Yes. Because what was in the Hadley Corporation's best interest was opposed to my own best interest or at least the interest of what my dick wanted. I had actually toyed with the idea of keeping the factory open, juggling some numbers just to make her happy, to help this town and do some good. I couldn't do it. I was raised better than that, by a single mom who suffered a lot and never put her own selfish wants above her duty to others. I owed it to myself to uphold my integrity, to be honest and aboveboard even if it meant making the personal sacrifice of not getting to be with Maggie. Which sounded fine and sensible until I saw her again.

The sight of her in a tight yellow t-shirt that hugged her ample breasts was enough to make my mouth water and my knees go week.

A guy next to me said hello.

"I'm Luke. The girl on the end there is my wife Sarah Jo. You're here with Maggie?"

"I'm not *with* Maggie. She invited me here," I said, grumbling.

"The cheerleaders are all independent women, trust me. My wife used to run the lumberyard. Nobody bosses these girls around. It takes a strong man to win one over."

"I don't have a chance, man. I work for Hadley."

"The corporation, not the plant," he nodded. "Everybody in this town knows who you are and why you're here. I guarantee you if you shut that plant down, she'll be the first one lighting a torch to come after you."

"Tar and feather me?" I said, making a bad chicken joke that got the frown it deserved from Luke.

We made polite small talk for a few minutes before the girls started to make a lot of noise.

"Now, the girls are hilarious once they get going here. The other team will about crap themselves over some of the stuff they say. It's beautiful. I mean, it's not elegant, so you gotta get over that if you have any hang-ups about women acting like ladies and shit."

"Nah. I had a single mom. She'd stop working long enough to beat my ass if I said anything that stupid," I said. "Plus, I like that Maggie isn't afraid to speak her mind. It's just not that simple."

He nodded. "You have to decide what's important."

"I know what my job is here," I said.

"I'm not sure you get it. You may think I'm a total stranger, but we have a lot in common."

"People in small towns sure are friendly," I deadpanned.

"Tell me when I'm wrong. You're good at your job and pride yourself on doing it well. You don't know why you can't leave this woman alone, but she's all you think about. There are at least three very practical reasons to walk away from her and not look back, like major reasons that screw up your life and hers. Now we get to the part that if you go for it with her, then you're letting a lot of people down as well as your own sense of duty and honor."

"What are you, CIA or some shit? Seriously that was creepy. How did you do that?"

Luke laughed. "You have to tell her how you feel about her. Admit it to her."

"I'm not in love with her. It's just lust."

"Oh, you're still stuck in that stage?" Luke shook his head. "Call me in a week then."

"In a week I should be done here and long gone."

"That's what you think, buddy," he said.

Luke got up to go talk to an older man holding a baby in a sunhat on his knee. He picked up the baby and kissed her chubby cheeks. He had a daughter with Sarah Jo. There was no damn reason that should make my chest hurt.

The game was getting started, co-ed teams from the chicken plant and a fish plant over on the other side of Pendleton. The Feathers wore yellow shirts and had a mascot, some poor bastard in a ratty chicken suit that looked like Big Bird had been on a drunken bender. The fish stick team wore blue shirts, and their mascot didn't look any better, some guy with blue knee socks and sneakers on with a baggy fish suit that went to his knees, his face sticking out between the flapping fake gills. It was a total shit show right down to the local troop of scouts hawking unsold cookies that were about to expire. Why had I agreed to this?

After a few rounds of goofy cheers that shouldn't have made me smile, but did, Maggie walked over to Luke and took the baby from him. I took one look at her holding that baby and fled for the concession stand. I bought a snow cone, not caring what flavor. I just had to get my eyes off her holding a chubby-cheeked infant and beaming. It did things to me. I shoveled shaved ice in my mouth as a girl in overalls and a yellow shirt walked up.

"Hey, you should come sit with us. I saw you clapping a beat earlier. You're qualified."

"I work for Hadley," I blurted out like an idiot.

"I know who the hell you are," she said. "I'm Layla. Health department counselor, vintage clothing lover, sex toy expert. At your service."

"I've never had a sex toy expert at my service. I don't believe I require your services, but it was nice meeting you."

"I'm Maggie's friend. She deserves better," she said flatly.

"I'm not going to argue with that," I said.

"Good. Awareness is the first step to rehabilitation. You have potential," she said.

"To what, join the cheerleaders?" I asked.

"To be good enough for her. She's the hardest worker I know, and one of the most loyal friends you'll ever met. You'd be lucky to get her," she said.

"Unfortunately my job here doesn't allow me to be good enough or lucky enough to get to be with her."

"Then, Mr. Leeds, it is most certainly your loss."

Layla shook her head at me and then started to walk away. She stopped, turned around and gave me the finger. I chuckled. Returning to my seat, I saw Maggie and her friends laughing. They knew how to have a good time. The game went eleven long innings of Maggie and her friends firing increasingly hilarious heckles and cheers at the teams and me sweating through my clothes just from looking at her. God, that shirt should come with a warning label. I felt like I could see straight through it.

The Feathers lost, and Sarah Jo stood up and announced that we were all invited back to Cecil's for the Loser's Lounge after-party. I was ready to pass on that and go get in another workout, maybe blow off some tension. Then Maggie showed up at my side and hooked her arm through mine.

"You gotta come to Loser's Lounge. Get the full experience. How can we win you over if you slink off to pout in your hotel room?" she laughed. "Come on!"

She rode over with her friends, and I parked down the block from Cecil's. The place was packed with factory people, players and spectators. Families with kids sitting in the grill area, Loser's Lounge over by the big TV's on the other side of the bar. Baskets of wings and platters of chips and queso were passed around, and a huge bread bowl of artichoke dip came out. I made a beeline for it unapologetically. It was delicious, just the right amount of garlic. I was gobbling it happily when Sarah Jo came over.

"You know my husband whipped that up just for you. The queso here is the best, but he heard you liked artichokes," she said.

"So he *is* a spy," I teased.

"We all are. We're on the same side. We want our town to stay prosperous and wholesome and good."

"And I'm on the dark side?"

"Apparently, although I'm not sure Maggie's convinced of that. You should talk to her."

"No, she's asked me to stay away."

"That's because she's loyal to a fault. She thinks it's a betrayal to family, factory, and the flag to consort with the enemy. But once upon a time, I was up the same creek. Now I've got Luke and baby makes three."

"Are you two like the walking billboard for forbidden love?"

"Yes. We've thought about putting it on the sign at the city limits. Home of the Hadley Chicken Processing Plant and Forbidden Romance."

"Catchy," I said.

"Trust me, dude, breaking the rules is a lot more fun than toeing the line. Nobody's going to thank you for giving up your own happiness."

She walked off in a trail of unsolicited advice and left me hunched over the artichoke dip and scanning the crowd for Maggie. There she was, bright and laughing, high-fiving the friend who'd flipped me off earlier. I stepped away from the dip and went right over to them, interrupting.

"Great game today," I said.

"We lost," she said.

"I wasn't talking about the score. I liked the enthusiasm, the infectious cheer."

"Not a softball fan?"

"My first game. You initiated me," I said, every word laden with meaning.

"I'll leave you two to talk... sports," Layla said archly and went for more wings.

Maggie passed me a plastic cup. "We're all having one. It's the official drink of the Loser's Lounge. Rum and cola."

"What's the official drink when you win?" I said.

"Same, but we put cocktail umbrellas in them and shout a lot," she said. I laughed.

"I've missed you."

"I'm right here," she said, finishing her nachos and sipping her drink.

"So you celebrate whether you win or lose?"

"Yeah, we're for the team no matter what. Together in triumph and defeat alike."

"So, the one with the overalls that flipped me off—,"

"Layla, and I'm sure you deserved it," she put in.

"I wouldn't argue that. Anyway, I was wondering if you'd like to get out of here. Go have dinner."

"I thought we settled this," she said, her eyes too bright for mere exasperation.

"Does it feel like we have?" I challenged. She shook her head.

"There's a place over in Pendleton that has the best Indian butter chicken you've ever tasted," she offered.

"Well, if you're trying to evangelize me into loving this town too much to shut the factory, you really should show me the sights. Including the best Indian restaurant around," I said teasingly.

"Let's go," she said.

"I'll drive. I haven't had anything to drink but water," I said.

"I had half a rum and cola and a ton of wings. I'm good," she said.

"Good," I said. "Still driving though."

"It's like you don't trust me."

"Nope, I'm afraid it's all a ploy to drop me in the middle of nowhere and make me find my way back."

"Damn, you read my mind."

I drove us to the restaurant, and we squeezed in at a high table in the crowded room. We gave our orders to the waitress, and Maggie started ripping into the naan. Her mood seemed to have shifted a bit since her flirtatious comments at the bar. I wasn't sure what had changed on the ride over.

"Are you carbo-loading for later activities?" I quipped, trying to lighten the mood.

She frowned. "I'm stress-eating. It stresses me out to look at you."

"Because I'm hot?" I deadpanned.

"Exactly!" she said too loudly. "And because you're a horrible human being. You're a stuck-up city boy who thinks you're better than us. You'd rather get more profits for your shitty corporation than protect the welfare of an entire community, a community that welcomed you despite who you are," she said. She was ranting a little, waving her hands around. I tried not to laugh.

"Couple of points here," I said. "One, it isn't my corporation. If I owned it, somebody else would be here doing this crappy job. Two, it's not what I'd rather do, It's what I have an obligation to do. What I'd rather do is forget dinner and go straight to dessert. And by 'dessert' I mean teaching you a thing or ten with your legs over my shoulders. So don't act like you know everything about me."

"But you do think you're better than us," she said, pouting a bit.

"No. But I know my duty, and I take pride in doing the right thing."

"Pride keeping you warm at night?" she joked.

"No. But I'm not sleeping that great," I admitted. "I'm not cold, me and my pride. I'm blazing hot because I'm thinking about you. Because as soon as I lie down at night, on those pretty white sheets you put there, the first thing I do—do you want to hear this?" I said, having a sudden pang of maybe offending her.

"Yeah, yeah I want to hear it," she said, nodding vigorously. Her eyes were suddenly dark, her pupils dilated.

"As soon as I lie down, all I can see is you. You behind the desk the first night I saw you, and you with that hair falling all over my hands when I kissed you, and dancing at the potluck. All of it rushes in on me, and I'm so hard in an instant that going to sleep is impossible. There's no chance."

"So what do you do?" she said a little breathlessly.

I left her in suspense while the food was delivered. The incredible, fragrant dish caught my attention, and I started eating what was undoubtedly the best butter chicken on earth. She kicked me under the table. "Then what do you do?" she said insistently.

"You realize that I haven't been able to get you off my mind for a single minute since we met," I said.

"Maybe that's my plan. Distract you so you can't do your job," she snarked, chasing the last of the sauce around her plate with a piece of naan.

"Then you're very good at it. Because I'm completely distracted by you," I said.

"You are impossible," she said, throwing her scrap of naan on the plate. "I can't sit here and banter with you and not like it. I get so wound up,. This was the worst idea."

"It was literally your idea," I said.

"No, you were the one who said we should get out of there and go to dinner," she grumbled, drinking some of her water.

"Fine, I'll take the blame," I said.

"Good. You should."

"But you have to admit your part in this too," I told her.

She scoffed. "And what do you think my part is?" she asked.

"The part where you make me so hard I have to stroke

my own damn cock until I come like a horny teenager every fucking night just to get a hour or two of fitful sleep. And then again in the shower in the morning because I can't get you out of my goddamn head."

She stared at me for a moment, unblinking. Then, suddenly, her hand shot in the air as she called the waitress for our check. After I threw a few bills on the table, she grabbed my hand and nearly dragged me out of the restaurant.

In the car, I glanced at her before I pulled away from the parking spot.

"My house," was all she said.

I nodded. Somehow, neither of us could bear to speak. The tension between us was so thick, so heady that words failed us. I drove that car with one hand on her knee. I was breathing hard all the way back to town, all the way to the turn onto the quiet street where she lived. Then I found that I'd forgotten how to breathe at all. She was so beautiful, so ready to be mine. I tried to make my hands stop shaking. All that pent-up desire, all the fury of want I'd been keeping leashed—I had to go slow, be gentle with her. I couldn't unleash that explosive arousal. She'd be terrified, too stunned to even respond.

When I stopped in front of her house, I cut the ignition and turned to her. Even in the darkness, the soft light from her porch seeming faraway, I could see her wide eyes, expectant and excited. I could see the pale, trembling hand as it settled over mine. She seemed as breathless as I felt.

"Let's go inside," she said.

13

MAGGIE

His eyes were so dark, so fiery, I felt like they could devour me, swallow me whole. I felt a shiver almost of fear on the edge of my anticipation. I could barely walk straight on my way to unlock the door, although I was sober as could be. The warm breeze ruffled through my ponytail as I tried twice to fit my key into the lock, clumsy with desire. He put his hand on my wrist to steady me.

As if his touch would calm me.

I shook harder. Everything inside me was zinging around wildly in excitement and panic all at once. I turned around and looked at him, helpless. He took the key from me and opened the door smoothly as if it wasn't impossible to do.

Once inside the door, the keys jangling into their bowl on the hall table, I reached for him. I was too late. Jeremiah already had his hands on me, dragging me against him. I didn't have a chance to catch my breath or hold on to him. He swept me into a kiss, breathtaking and intense.

Jeremiah's rough fingertips traced my jaw and slid down my sensitive neck. I shivered under his hands, knowing he'd make me shiver a hundred more times before he made me scream. I wanted that so much, and at the same time wanted the kiss to go on forever, never stopping. Firecrackers seemed to spark and pop behind my eyes as his tongue pushed into my mouth, merciless, demanding. I felt a sob rising in my throat when his big hand cupped my breast. I arched into him, pressing my nipple into his palm, wanting more.

"All this time I've wanted you, my beautiful Maggie," he groaned against my neck as he licked and sucked. Every suck sent trails of sparks zinging down my skin and left me drenching and quivering.

"Please," I said, because it was all I could manage to say.

I pulled back, staggering out of his embrace for an instant. I pointed toward my bedroom like a bad pantomime and made to lead the way. He reached out and swept me up into his arms. He had me in the bedroom in seconds, on the bed, stripping off my shirt. I stretched my arms above my head, unprepared for him to throw the shirt while bearing me down onto the bed, his mouth fastened on my nipple through the lace of my bra. The lace was cheap and rough, a jagged counterpoint to his hot, wet mouth on my pebbling skin. I moaned, clasping his head to my breast urgently. His hand worked over my other breast, fondling and squeezing, pinching the nipple into aching hardness. Every sharp pinch made me shriek with spikes of pleasure. I wanted his cock inside me. I felt like I couldn't wait another second. I needed him plunging and thrusting, rutting into me immediately.

Then, just as I was about to suggest that he bury his hard cock inside me, he slid down my body, mouthing the curve of my belly before I could suck in my stomach. He unbuttoned my jeans. I couldn't describe the jolt I felt as his fingers brushed low on my belly and then he unzipped my jeans, pushed them down. I couldn't take my eyes off his hands, the way his fingers stole into my lace panties, cupped my mound. God, he was going to feel how wet I was, what a slick, fevered mess I was down there. His fingers moving through my folds felt so good, so slippery and sexy that I ground my hips into him, trying to get his fingers inside me at least. I tossed my head back and forth, gripped the bedspread in my fists just to hold on to something. When he cupped my pussy, the heel of his hand pressing into my clit with a hard, relentless pressure, I started rocking instinctively. I was gasping and crying out already when he dipped his finger into my slit. My pussy convulsed around him, around that long, blunt finger as I pumped against his palm getting myself off. I screamed, coming apart with a sudden orgasm.

I didn't expect Jeremiah to follow up that fierce orgasm by ripping my panties off with his bare hands, but I felt the rip of the lace, felt him push my quivering thighs apart and bury his face between my legs. His tongue lapped at me, tasting me, the wetness of arousal there. He rubbed my clit furiously with the pad of his thumb, working it so hard and fast. His tongue slid into me as he teased my clit mercilessly, sending me over the edge again, sobbing this time because I didn't think I could take so much pleasure. I could die of it, of Jeremiah Leeds eating me out on my own bed. My bare legs tossed and jerked around his dark head buried between my pale thighs. It was the sexiest thing I'd ever seen, ever felt.

He licked his lips, raised his head and came to gather me in his arms. "God you taste good," he growled.

I about died of gratitude. It was so considerate of him to give me a few minutes while I recovered from not one, but two bed-rattling orgasms. He was so tender, not at all like I expected him to be—selfish and goal-oriented. Jeremiah Leeds had hidden depths.

"I need a few minutes," I said, my breath seeming to return to my body, which continued to tingle. I felt lit up from the inside, like all that pleasure and cherishing had made me glow.

Slowly, as I came back to myself, I stroked his chest. I pushed his shirt up to reveal the rock-hard abs I'd guessed at but never touched. He let me stroke his stomach, his chest, before he reached behind his head, grabbed his shirt and dragged it off. I had all that man, well-muscled, his body so different from mine in its shape and size and texture—all mine for the taking. My mouth watered at the thought. I ran my lips across his chest, feeling his hot skin, the crinkle of his chest hair. I rubbed my body against his, catlike, savoring the feeling of his smooth skin and his heat and hardness.

I wanted that so much, had wanted it for a long time, the yielding of my soft curves to the hard planes of his body, the relentless strength, the brutal beauty of him. I wanted to join with him in the most primitive way. I ran my hands along him, murmuring words of admiration, my mouth on his shoulder, his neck. He caught my chin in his hand and held me still to kiss me. The force of that kiss rocked me back. My shoulders were flat on the mattress, Jeremiah above me. My arms went around him, my palms savoring the hot, smooth skin of his muscled back. The heavy bulk of him pressed me deep into the bed, threatened to smother me in the best, most delicious way. I craved the weight of his body on mine, relished it on a primal level. I wriggled beneath him gloriously, feeling the bump and rub of every part of him against me.

His tongue was in my mouth and it was so sensuous and

demanding and unhurried in a tormenting way. As if he had all the time in the world to explore every curve and hollow of my body. That there was no rush at all, like he had the iron control of some kind of superhuman. The sensations he made riot through my body were already driving me wild again. It took all my concentration and strength to spread my legs apart just a few inches. It was hard to focus when he was kissing me like the devil himself, wicked and slow, teasing, stroking, making me want to scream in bliss and frustration alike.

Gripping his thick biceps felt incredible, all that power under my hands, harnessed by his will into gentleness and taunting sensuality. He nipped at my lips, slid his knee between my legs. The pressure he gave me with his thigh was at the same time a relief and infuriatingly not enough. I needed all of him, his powerful length pushing deep into me, making me spread my legs wide just to try to take him inside me. My pussy pulsed at the thought, the image of his cock disappearing into my body. Oh, how I wanted to feel the heavy invasion of it within me, the pressure of his pounding thrusts. I could have wept with wanting it. I writhed against him, trying to hurry him, to increase the pressure of his maddeningly gentle touch.

"You like that?" he said, his thigh going harder against my damp sex. I nodded furiously in case he wasn't sure I meant 'yes'.

"How about this?" he said, his mouth fastening onto my nipple.

I jerked in pleasure, my fingers in his hair, trying to trap him there with his questing, wet mouth velvety as it consumed my sensitive flesh. I bucked under him or tried to, pinned down by the delicious weight of him. Slowly, tenderly he worked my nipple, swirling his tongue in a slow circle around it, brushing the tip of his tongue over it, sweeping the flat of his hot tongue back and forth. I clenched, gritted my teeth, tried to endure it, sure it would burn me up into cinders. The slow, deliberate tenderness threatened to undo me, to make me lose my mind. His teeth scraped my sensitive, aching nipple and made me jerk at the edge of pain that sharpened my pleasure. He moved his mouth lazily to the other nipple and worked it over just the same, building the ecstasy till I was ready to scream and beg. Then he moved back up to my mouth and kissed me deeply, deftly. Our lips fit together perfectly, a gorgeous, perfect kiss that was equal parts sex and romance. I never once forgot, even with my eyes shut tight, that Jeremiah was the man kissing me. It was no faceless fantasy man, but Jeremiah himself. The enemy. The man set to destroy everything I held dear. His hand was working between my legs like he planned to spend at least two months just petting me to distraction. I'd go insane in less than five minutes it was so good. Too good.

"I need you," I whispered roughly. "Please. All of you."

"You want that?" he said, his lips against mine.

"Yes. S—so much," I stuttered. He withdrew his wicked fingers at my words.

It seemed to unleash him.

This time, he moved his body between my thighs. He levered up on his hands, eyes bright and locked on mine. He brushed my cheek with his fingers, then kissed my lips softly. I trembled in anticipation, my arms around his neck. I held my breath, bracing myself for the hard first thrust, the explosion that waited after all that patience.

I was shocked when I felt the massive hardness of his erection press tenderly at my sensitive sex, breaching me for a long, slow thrust that left me taut with tension, panting and sobbing at the gentleness with which he wielded that power. His broad, manly shoulders above me gave me something to grip. Before I knew it, my hips were arching up off the bed, wanting to take him in, wanting the slick push of his cock within me, wanting him to go harder, deeper, give me every inch of him.

"Please," I gasped, "don't hold back. Let me feel you."

"I don't want to hurt you," he said, his voice tight with control.

"Jeremiah," I managed, "I want to feel all of you. Please," I said, babbling a little in my urgency.

With a jerk of his hips he thrust all the way into me, every long, thick inch until I thought I'd lose my mind from the pressure, the feeling of fullness. I closed my eyes, imagining him spearing into my body, the slickness of my juices easing his way. I bucked my hips to meet his thrusts. He was careful, giving me short, shallow thrusts at first, but I urged him on, taking more and more, craving it after that first, maddening deep push. Then he gave it to me, all of it, pumping into me almost wildly. The corded muscles of his arms stood out under my grip as he drove into me. Every plunge made me growl, some guttural, deep sound of satisfaction that I could take all of him. The roar he gave when he came hot and hard inside me was a sound I could never forget. He gave a shudder and his arms gave way. He collapsed onto me and I held him, breathless, the wet rush from his climax still in me. I felt a flutter of pleasure at the primal way I possessed him, exhausted from his orgasm, still half-hard within me, the slickness between my legs proof that he had given me all of himself, every drop. I gloried in it.

"You feel fucking perfect," he gasped, rolling off of me.

I almost cried out at the immediate feeling of emptiness

as he withdrew from me.

"God, you're amazing," he said, his mouth on mine, kissing me deeply.

When his hand brushed the side of my breast, I responded, arching, pressing my breast into his palm eagerly.

"Want more, do you?" he said slyly.

"I've never felt so good before," I said, before drifting off to peaceful sleep.

When I woke up hours later, he was still in bed with me. His arm was around me, my head pillowed on his chest. I let myself lay there and bask in it, in waking up in his arms and remembering the life-changing sex we'd had. I let my eyes drift shut and smiled blissfully until he kissed me awake softly.

"Want breakfast?" he asked.

"I need a shower," I said, scrunching up my face.

"You go shower. Make it fast or you'll have company," he teased.

It felt so good to be teasing and playful and affectionate with him. I kissed his cheek and darted off to shower. In just a few minutes, I was clean and dressed and in the kitchen, where he was slicing fruit. The Company Man was cutting up a kiwi in my kitchen. It was the weirdest thing that had ever happened, except for the equally strange fact that it made me happy. I went up and hugged him. We made pancakes and had some fruit and cracked my emergency champagne for mimosas. It was a great way to start the day.

"I want to take you out tonight," he said.

"Shouldn't we keep this quiet? I mean, there's a pretty clear conflict of interests," I protested.

"We have nothing to hide. I'm happy to be seen with you, Maggie," he said. That settled that.

JEREMIAH

Dinner at a local barbecue joint was something terrific when it was with Maggie. She seemed so much more relaxed. She was at ease with me, and when I slid in beside her in the booth instead of sitting across from her, she held my arm and leaned her head on my shoulder. I liked having her at arm's reach, so I could hold her, kiss her, know she hadn't changed her mind and run off.

I convinced her to take me sightseeing on Sunday. She picked me up at the B&B.

"You have on hiking boots. Should I have gone to a sporting goods store?" I asked.

"Oh, we're just gonna tour the factory," she said lightly.

"You're kidding."

"Yeah, I am. I just wanted to remind you why we're total enemies still. Because you're the big city stiff who wants to shut down the plant. It would serve you right if I made you take an up-close tour of the scalding vats," she teased.

"I've already evaluated those."

"Oh. That's a total spoiler. It would be a rerun if I took

you there. Guess I'll have to drive you out to some of my favorite spots nearby. There's loads of scenic hiking trails…"

"Perfect for hiding a body?" I joked.

"Exactly," she said with a laugh. "But I was thinking more like we'd take a walk and have a picnic."

"Did you pack one? Because all I really have is the minibar back at the room."

"Yeah, I did. It's in the back. But listen, this place is so beautiful. You're going to love it. You're going to want to sell your place in the city and move here," she said enthusiastically.

"Is that what you want? For me to move here?" I asked. She blushed and kept her eyes on the road. I wanted her to say yes. That she wanted me to live there, that she wanted to have me close by for potluck dinners and wild sex and making breakfast together. But she didn't say a word.

"It's about fifteen miles out of town, between here and Pendleton but out to the west."

"What's there?"

"It's just a place I like. You can see the mountains. There's a spring."

"So it's like Little House on the Prairie?"

"No. There are no mountains out on the prairie," she said. "You city boys, I swear." I chuckled.

"You'll have to educate me then," I said.

"Is everything innuendo with you?" she asked in mock exasperation.

"Apparently everything with *you* is innuendo since you think it's all sexual."

"It is. It's all sexual," she said grimly. "I mean clearly I don't like spending time with you at all. We only see each other in the dark for ten minutes of fornicating."

"No barbecue. No sightseeing. No making each other

laugh. Yeah, it's nothing but sexual," I said sarcastically. She smiled at me. She had a killer smile.

We made our way out of town, and she parked on some old farm road and got out and handed me a reusable grocery bag with pictures of eggplants all over it. I looked at it suspiciously.

"What? Who has picnic baskets nowadays? This was the bag I had," she said and struck out walking.

I caught up to her as we climbed a hill and then another. After the third, we came to a creek with crystalline water surrounded by huge boulders. She chose one in the sun and took the bag from me. While she unpacked food, I couldn't help but look around and see how beautiful it was.

"So, great picnic spot, right?"

"Yes," I said, sitting down beside her.

I took her face in my hands and kissed her. She took my breath away, her openness, her generosity. She reached for me, wrapped her arms around my waist as I kissed her. I could have lived in that moment for the rest of my life, the fresh breeze, the view of the creek and the mountains far beyond, the woman in my arms. It made me want to build a home in that spot, some pioneer impulse to erect a homestead with my own two hands, to sit on a porch and watch the sunrise in this exact spot with my arm around her every damn morning. It was such a powerful impulse that I was speechless. This place, this woman, a chance to build something permanent instead of being a nomad traveling around destroying factories and entire towns. A way out, a new path. An idea I had never imagined before.

But I kept that all to myself. I sank down onto the quilt she'd spread and listened to her talk about playing out in that creek with her cousins and friends when she was a kid.

"Layla acts fearless now, but she was scared of the

minnows getting her toes. I was afraid of snakes, but she'd hunt for those and chase them with a stick. Minnows though—it's hilarious. We would come out here in the summer, if we could get a ride, and just splash in the creek till we were soaked and then dry off in the sun. Make daisy chains with the wild clover and blow dandelions. It was regular Hallmark stuff, so pretty and peaceful. Except for the time I ripped open my leg chasing my cousins across the rocks. They had to carry me to a farmhouse for help."

"Were you seriously hurt? Did you need stitches?"

"No. It just scared the crap out of me. I was dramatic for a nine-year-old. So two of my cousins carried me. The lady at the farm patched me up with band-aids and let us play with the baby goats. Little known fact about me. I love baby goats. I watch those YouTube videos where they wear pajamas and play on little toddler slides and stuff. Cheers me right up."

I laughed. "Baby goats in pajamas? Is this something people do?"

"Yeah, and they film it. It's Internet gold. I mean, it's super cuteness. I'll pull some up on my phone later, see if you're not hooked," she said.

"I'm hooked on you," I blurted.

"That was so cheesy," she laughed, but she looked pleased.

"You know you love it when I'm cheesy," I replied.

"Yeah, I kinda do," she said and kissed my cheek.

"What if we could do better than videos?" I said.

"What do you mean?"

"Well, we have a couple options. One, you could throw yourself off the rocks so I could carry my injured girlfriend to the nearby farms for medical aid and goats, or we could just walk up to the places and ask if we can look around."

"You mean knock on their doors?" she said.

"Yeah. Exactly. Look, Maggie, I didn't get where I am in the corporate world by being scared to knock on a door," I said in mock seriousness.

"You mean the corporate world where you live in a hotel, drive a rental car and shut stuff down? Wow, sounds fabulous, I should knock on more doors," she said sarcastically.

"Hey, don't get salty," I said, kissing her briefly. "All I'm saying is, if you love baby goats that much, we're in the neighborhood of a several farms that seemed to have animals and it's in my power to find you some goats to pet or hold or whatever it is you do with goats."

"I would freaking LOVE to pet goats today. Like, next to you not shutting down the factory obviously."

"Yeah, you gotta needle me with that, remind me I'm the bad guy," I rolled my eyes.

"Just don't want you to forget."

I shook my head. "Trust me, there's no danger of that."

We drank the sparkling cider she'd packed and ate the cheese and crackers. I convinced her to stretch out on the quilt with me and look up at the sky.

"I haven't done this since I was a kid," she said, her head on my shoulder. "Looking for pictures in the clouds and stuff."

"I never did this. You don't exactly lie down on the sidewalk in the city to look at the sky. We didn't have roof access in our building. You could only see snatches of sky. Tyler, my brother, he loves working outdoors. He had a rough time, only survivor of a roadside explosive device. Being outside in the open seems to help him. I can see why. I'm not, like, a trauma survivor or anything, but fresh air and space just feels good."

"Look at you, talking about your feelings, Company Man," she teased. "It's the sunshine and the clouds. It changes your outlook. I think I managed to take the city out of the city boy. Victory!" she said. "You're going to want to move here and play with goats."

"You're adorable."

"It's the red hair. Very Princess Merida. I can't help it," she joked.

"I mean it. Not just your hair. It's your personality. You're energetic and smart and it's no wonder that all these workers want you to look after their kids while they're at work. You're loyal and responsible and—"

"Total Girl Scout? Gotta say, that description makes me sound like a terrific babysitter next door. But it's not gonna play that well on my online dating profile."

"Are you still on an app?" I asked, feeling myself frown.

"Nope. You?"

"No. It wouldn't make sense. I travel too often."

"Oh. I see," she said wryly. "You're a rolling stone. Gather no moss or girlfriends."

"I seem to have gathered one on this trip."

She looked at me. "Gathered what? A little bit of moss?" she joked.

"I'm serious, Maggie. You're more to me than some hook up. You have to know that. I've been trying to tell you all day that I care about you," I said.

"That's great, Jeremiah. But we live in the real world last I checked and you're fixing to take down the industry that supports my business and my community. We're taking this crazy attraction for a spin, but don't go reading too much into it. I've never been the kind of girl who could do a casual, one-night thing. I'm still not, but I'm trying to be sensible. This isn't going anywhere. It's a holiday affair. I mean—we want completely different things. We're opposites, and not in the rom-com way. In the doomed from the start way," she said.

I lay there, her head on my shoulder, and heard that she believed what she was saying. That my protest that I had feelings for her had flown right by her. I had thought, mistakenly, that she might want more than a fling. I'd shrug it off. She was right. I was a man who gathered no moss. Which should have been a relief instead of leaving me feeling lonely and irritable, which was where I was.

"So, let's pack up and see if we can find ourselves some goats," I said, sitting up. I wasn't going to let one sour exchange ruin a good day. We had such a short amount of time together it would be stupid to waste it with a bad mood.

Soon we had set off down the rocky hill to the nearest farm, a tidy collection of whitewashed outbuildings around a gray farmhouse. There was a woman out by the hen house with a couple of kids.

"Good afternoon," I said. "I'm Jeremiah, and this is Maggie. We're out for a picnic and wondered if you had any goats on your property."

"Not to eat. For the picnic," Maggie giggled.

The woman smiled. "I'm Heather, and these two are Braden and Kaden, the twins." She indicated a pair of blond headed boys who were quite carefully scattering corn for the chickens.

"Good to meet you," I said. "My friend grew up around here and told me how she got to pet the goats at a neighboring farm when she was a kid. I got the idea to come and ask if you keep goats."

"That's so romantic. Back when we were dating, John, my husband got me the cutest little rabbit at the state fair.

Like us, it's settled down and started breeding. We have a rabbit hutch out back if you like to pet bunnies. We have cows and chickens, but we don't keep goats. You're welcome to visit the bunnies, though. Kaden loves them."

I looked at Maggie who nodded eagerly.

"So, it's all farm animals then?" I teased. She was beaming, it was irresistible, "We'd love to see your bunnies if Kaden would be our guide. Now, I don't know much about rabbits, Kaden. What do I need to know before I pet one?"

"Don't poke them in the eyes," he said solemnly. "Hold them gentle, and don't drop them. They like to nibble on lettuce, but don't poke it in their mouth. They don't like that."

"Good advice," I said. "I'll keep it in mind."

"Don't try to look at their butt. They'll kick you," Braden chimed in. Maggie laughed.

"Braden," his mom admonished.

"It's true!" he insisted. We laughed.

"I run a daycare in town," Maggie explained. "Anything to do with butts or underwear is sure-fire humor around me."

"Oh, you must be the one who runs Fun Factory. I remember seeing that go up in town when I was still working at the salon. It's a cute little place. What's going to happen to it now?"

"We don't know. But my friend Jeremiah here is the Hadley inspector who's been sent to shut us down."

"Way to toss me under the bus there, Mag," I said wryly. "Yes, Heather, I work for Hadley. I'm here to assess the viability of keeping the factory here or relocating overseas. And to pet bunnies, as well."

Carefully Kaden—or Braden—unlatched the hutch and took out a bunny. It was a little brown lop-eared creature that he handed to Maggie. She nestled it in her arms and whispered to it, stroking its fur with one finger, "Oh, they're precious," she said as the kids each got out a bunny to hold and show off.

"This one has a white paw. We call her White Paw," one of the twins said. I nodded, listening as the kids told us about the rabbits while their mother watched them proudly.

After we had admired the bunnies and discovered that 'bunnies have very many babies so fast' from one of the twins, we thanked them and said goodbye.

"Over on north of here, about two miles you'll find the Prescotts and they have goats. Some of them are show goats," Heather said.

We set off toward the promised goat farm. Maggie held my hand as we walked.

"Show goats? Are they singers and dancers?" I said.

"Stripper goats. Like showgirls," Maggie quipped. "But they prefer to be called burlesque goats. It's more dignified."

"Will there be sequin goat pajamas?"

"Tassels," she giggled.

We walked along until we reached the second farm. It was even prettier than the first, with a stretch of white fencing around the property and some horses in one pasture. It was a larger operation, more machinery and large sheds instead of the quaint henhouse and rabbit hutch we'd seen earlier. We went to the first shed we came to, and an older man directed us to the house where his wife and daughter-in-law were setting up a lemonade stand with the kids.

"This is idyllic," I said, "look at this." The card table with the neat white cloth, the crooked, crayon drawn sign advertising fresh lemonade for fifty cents, the two women helping the four or five kids arrange cups and napkins without spilling anything.

"I think it's making me thirsty," Maggie said. "They're so cute."

"You just want to butter them up so they'll show you the goats," I accused.

"Maybe," she grinned.

We bought lemonade, introduced ourselves and got permission to meet the goats.

"Adeline, our oldest, shows pygmy goats with 4-H, so we've got plenty if you want to see them," the woman said. She and the kids took us out to the neatly kept pen.

"Oh my God!" Maggie squealed. "They're so cute! I've never held a pygmy goat. I've just seen them on YouTube."

"We have a channel. Our goats are on it," the mother offered. "It's part of Adeline's project."

"I am subscribing to that tonight," Maggie vowed. She was excited, shifting her weight from foot to foot, beaming like a kid about to shout 'gimme gimme' about the goats.

They really were tiny and cute looking with wee grouchy faces. We petted the goats, especially around the nubs of their horns where we were told they liked it. I whipped out my phone and took pictures of Maggie in her version of heaven—surrounded by noisy and playful pygmy goats. Damned if I didn't want to buy the woman a goat. I shook my head at my own foolishness. While she and the kids played with the animals, I headed back to the shed and spoke to the farmer who owned the spread, asked him a few questions about the growing season, weather, and soil acidity. I made notes in my phone and thanked him. Then I collected Maggie who had gone in the farmhouse to wash her hands.

All the way back to the car, I was lost in thought. She

chattered on about how happy she was, what a great day it had been. I held her hand and wondered exactly what the hell I was going to do.

That night I reviewed all the numbers on the factory. I ran the spreadsheets again, worked up a couple more projections. It was troubling but clear. It wasn't cost-effective to keep the plant in operation. Even though so many businesses and people I'd come to know depended on it for their livelihood. The nursery and florist, the daycare, the hardware store and restaurants and a dozen other places. And Maggie. Maggie relied on that factory's workers. She'd lose her business. There was no way around it. I couldn't save it. No matter how much it meant to her or how much she meant to me.

After three hours of wasted effort trying from every angle to make the thing look profitable, I called my brother.

"What's up?" Tyler asked.

"The sky's falling, brother," I said. "I can't keep the factory open. Even though these people depend on it, and I care about them. I should never have gotten personally involved."

"You getting emotionally involved is the last thing I ever expected from you. I thought this was a standard job—go in, run the numbers, shut it down. What's different?"

"The girl. She runs a daycare that caters to factory workers. It's her entire business. And it's not the only one that relies on the factory."

"You're just realizing this now? That one major industry supports the rest of a small town? Dude, you're the one that went to college," he laughed at me. "And she must be something if she's got you rethinking numbers."

"This wasn't what I wanted to do with my life," I complained.

"So quit. Take it from me, shit doesn't turn out the way you planned. So change direction."

"I've worked long and hard to reach the level I'm in at Hadley," I argued.

"And you seem so happy with it," he said sarcastically. "Do what feels right. That's all I'm saying."

"Thanks for the advice. How are you doing?"

"Same as ever. It's all good," he said.

"Got a girlfriend yet?" I said. I was hesitant to ask, and I was basically talking in code. He'd had a lot of ill effects from his experience in the Marines, and it had messed up his head.

"No. But it sounds like you do."

"Get out there. Go on a date," I said. "What does your shrink say?"

"I'll go out with someone when I'm damn good and ready. I haven't seen a woman yet who interests me since I got back. The shrink says give it time, the mind and body heal slowly."

"How helpful," I said wryly.

"Yeah, these counselors don't give you the quick fix, I'll give them that. She said a support group might help, but I'm sick of talking about all this."

"Maybe give it a chance?" I suggested.

"Right. That's definitely a hobby I want to take up. Forget circuit training and working construction. I want to sit in a circle and talk about my feelings and fears, right, Jer?"

"It's what you've always dreamed of," I joked. "Isn't that why you enlisted?"

"It was mostly the signing bonus, but yeah, the chance to whine about my bad dreams to a lot of strangers with their own shit... definitely a life goal," Tyler said. "Now quit stressing out, decide what you want and go for it."

"You're a life coach now, Oprah?" I asked. After a bit more ball-busting, I hung up with Tyler.

I had known there was no one I could ask for advice that would tell me to walk away. I was torn between making the soundest recommendation to my employer and doing what was best for the community. The community and Maggie.

I had some soul searching to do.

There was the job I'd been hired to do. The clear recommendation.

That result happened to be the ultimate cockblock. The obstacle to a relationship with Maggie that could never be overcome.

Or I could turn in a very unethical recommendation to keep the plant open, save the town, probably get the girl and then get fired and the factory closed anyway when they sent someone else in to do what I couldn't. It was a lose-lose situation for everyone involved.

15

MAGGIE

Jeremiah asked me out to dinner, and I took him up on it. As soon as I was done at work, I rushed home to get ready. He picked me up and took me to Cecil's. It was my pick, because nobody had a better order of ribs in the state as far as I was concerned. Any man being evangelized to love this place needed only those dry rub ribs to melt off the bone and affect a change in his mind.

"These are life-altering ribs," I told him as we sat down. "They're going to sear all the darkness from your soul and leave you happy, full, and committed to saving any town that produces authentic dry-rub ribs of this quality. The process is so extensive they only fire up the smoker once a month to do these. You're lucky to be here."

"I know I'm a lucky man, although pork products didn't come to mind. I was thinking I'm glad to be out with you," he said.

"You've really been turning on the charm the last couple of days. You got a factory to save, too?" I teased.

"No, I've got a girl to win over. Despite my job, and the unfortunate way we met."

"You were checking in to my parents' B&B."

"And I tried to chat you up, but you learned my name and shut me right down," he said almost affectionately.

I wanted to keep things light, to forget about the feelings I was trying hard to ignore. Because I could talk about wanting to win him over to our town's side all I wanted, but in my heart that wasn't all I was wishing for. I was wishing for him to take one look at me and realize he could never do anything to hurt me, that he wanted to be with me more than he wanted to be a corporate Company man.

"Can you blame me?" I said. "My daycare center is fabulous. It breaks my heart to think of everything we could lose."

"So, ribs?" he changed the subject quickly. "Which sides do I want?"

"Potato salad, slaw, and the fried peaches. Trust me."

"I will," he said. We placed our order, and I went over to the bar to say hi to Sarah Jo.

"How's my favorite baby girl?" I said.

"Teething. Only at night. Kill me," Sarah Jo said, but she was grinning. "Looks like you're hanging out with the corporate spy after all. Was he worth all the angst?"

"The jury's still out on that," I hedged.

"You seem pretty sparkly and happy for someone who hasn't made up her mind. Look, if you like him, we'll like him. I promise."

"I thought if I brought him here for the ribs he might fall in love with the place and keep the plant open."

"That is a stupid plan, Mags, but considering how he's looking at you right now, you may have convinced him to fall in love with *something* around here," she teased.

"No way. He's not wired like that. Total city boy, travels

for work, no interest in settling down with the kick-ass chick who runs a daycare," I protested.

"You seem awfully sure about that. For a woman who's trying to woo him with ribs."

"I'm trying to win him over so he'll—"

"Like his dinner so much he decides to lose his job for falsifying reports? Get real, Maggie. You know how this is going to turn out. We all do. You're here with him because you want to be, and that's okay. Just let yourself enjoy it despite the factory situation," Sarah Jo said.

"Sometimes your no-nonsense attitude is a pain in the ass," I grumbled.

"Yeah, whatever. Love you," she said and went back to the kitchen to help out.

I slid back into the booth and met Jeremiah's eyes. He put down his phone and smiled at me.

"How is everyone?"

"Baby's teething. Sarah Jo had some dire predictions for me."

"Such as?"

"You'll close down the plant, and I should know that by now. That I was wasting my time trying to convince you to love this town," I blurted out.

"I don't consider what we have to be a waste of time. She's entitled to her opinion, but if she's going to make you feel badly—"

"Don't. She's my best friend and she's right. I should have quit after the potluck."

"Then you wouldn't have had mind-altering sex with me or petted the baby goats at that farm," he said.

"Don't be funny. It just makes things worse," I said miserably. "I'm smarter than this usually. I run my own business, very successfully I might add. So why did I have a blind spot when it came to you?"

"Probably the same reason I have one when it comes to you. Chemistry."

"Yeah. Chemistry. That must be it," I said ruefully.

Jeremiah looked so at home here. Leaned back in the booth, longneck in his hand, shirt open at the collar. Okay, so he looked like an expensive and much hotter than average person acting at home here in town. I could not let myself imagine that he'd consider staying even for a moment. But the temptation was so strong it made my teeth hurt from gritting them. He wouldn't move here, wouldn't stay because of me. I wasn't about to swallow my pride and ask. I was an independent woman, and I didn't beg unless an immediate orgasm was involved. The potential for future orgasms didn't count, not as a long-range plan and not as a reason to ask him for anything.

"The ribs are great, like you said."

"Great? They're phenomenal. You are damning with faint praise," I said.

"Says the woman who hasn't even tasted her dinner," he pointed out.

"I had things on my mind. And I like to anticipate things."

"I'll keep that in mind later, spend lots of time on the build-up for you," he said.

Just like that all the breath whooshed out of my stupid lungs. All I could think about was a slow, sensual, endless night between the sheets with Jeremiah Leeds.

Defiantly I swallowed hard and tried to eat my ribs. They seemed tasteless compared to the rich fantasy unspooling in my mind. I drank my Diet Coke and tried not to make crazy eyes at him and scare him while he ate. But I knew damn well where this was headed, and he'd better not be thinking about ordering dessert.

"I'm not that hungry," I said, clearing my throat.

"I thought you looked forward to this because you missed last month. You had to cover the late hours at the Fun Factory and Cooper got Fifths Disease which is really contagious—"

"You listen, that's for sure. So hear this. There's something I want more than the once a month ribs from paradise at Cecil's."

"Please say it's me and not more farm animals," he said.

"No, you smartass. I'd like to get out of here," I said boldly.

He went to the bar to settle the bill. I dashed to the ladies' room and hurried back, my lipstick fresh and ready to be kissed right off.

In the car, he reached for my hand and kissed it. It took me right back to the first time he had done that, how I felt the thrill through my whole body. It made my eyes sting a little at the recollection, how much it meant to me. And I wondered again why I was doing this. Why was I giving myself over again to something that was clearly going to break my heart in another week or two? How weak was I that I couldn't walk away?

At the B&B, he leaned over and whispered, "Do you want to go in separately? So you're not obviously going to my room?

"There's like ten rooms. Max is working the desk tonight. There's no point sneaking around," I said decisively. I reached over to open my door.

"Wait. That's my job," he said.

Jeremiah got out of the car and came around and opened my door. I barely got to my feet before I was in his arms. Swiftly, he pulled me to him, my head bent back over his arm for a Hollywood kiss. I was swept away in the stroke of his tongue, the urgency in his embrace. My knees were weak. I had to cling to him to stay upright as I answered his passionate kiss with my own.

By the time he drew back, I knew I was wild-eyed, kiss-swollen lips with lipstick smeared everywhere. I lifted myself on tiptoe to rub my lips against his sensuously. Jeremiah clasped me to him and kissed me again. We clung together for a long moment before we ventured into the lobby. He answered Max's greeting from the front desk, and I waved as we passed. No hiding my face tonight, no pretending I wasn't crazy about this man, as reckless as it was.

We climbed the stairs in lockstep, even our breath in sync. Inside the room, he shut the door, turned the deadbolt. The snick of the lock seemed to reverberate through my body, to shiver in my blood. We started peeling off our clothes without a word. There was no need for talking. I shimmied out of my panties while he reached behind his head and yanked his shirt off. I loved watching him do that, loved every inch of smooth skin revealed as he pulled the shirt up.

I had to get my hands on him. I touched his stomach, and he jerked as if startled. His eyes smoldered as they met mine. He grabbed my wrist and pressed my hand to his body, "You can touch all you want. It just feels electric," he said. His voice was husky and warm, curling through my body.

Greedy, I put both hands on him, unfastening his jeans and pushing them down. He helped me shuck off his jeans and boxers, and his hands went to my bra. Reaching behind me, he unfastened it so I could shrug out of it. I stood bare before him, not ashamed of my curves, just hungry to feel his touch. He didn't disappoint. He touched my breasts, reverently, tenderly at first, making my nipples pucker in anticipation. His fingers slowly curled toward them, making me breathless, eager. He rubbed them, rolled them between his thumb and forefinger, making a sharp jolt of pleasure jerk through me. I ran my hands up his muscular arms, reached up and pressed my lips to his shoulder and then bit it lightly. He growled low in his throat. He released my nipples to my whimper of dismay and caught me by the hips. He turned me around, bent me over the bed. A chill of excitement raced up my spine as his big hand stroked my back, pressed me down. His hands slid up and down my sides, stroked my bottom, my thighs, before his mouth was between my legs. I jerked, cried out as the tip of his tongue grazed the underside of my clit. The pleasure made my knees buckle, but his hands were there at my hips to hold me, my fists buried in the sheets.

He tongued me, sucked at my clit, pushed one and then two long fingers inside me, pressing and stroking my g-spot without mercy until I came and came, screaming, so fast and hard. I was still shuddering when he slid his fingers out of my quivering passage and got to his feet. I felt him there behind me, his thighs against mine, his bare, hot cock brushing against my sex. He rubbed the head of it over my wet slit, savoring the mess I'd made with a rumble of satisfaction in his throat. I was still sensitive from my orgasm, but I pushed my hips back toward him, taking the tip of his cock in me, taking him by surprise. He jerked forward, thrust into me slow and deep until I felt like I couldn't swallow. He was so deep inside me, filling me up. I needed to spread my legs more just to accommodate him, how thick, how rigid he was as he shoved it into my yielding flesh. I loved it, felt wild and powerful with that cock thrusting into me from behind. It gave me a shiver of bliss just thinking how we looked, me bent naked over the bed as he stood behind me, his palm on the small of my back, other hand on my hip, taking me.

His pace increased, his cock plunging into me faster, the brush of his balls against my flesh because he was going so deep, holding himself there, stirring inside me. I wanted it, wanted all of it and more. I craved this, the glorious surrender of it, the filthy knowledge that we were bent over a bed in my parents' inn, rutting like animals on the white sheets, moaning and screaming and writhing together. I slipped my hand down my stomach, pressed my fingers to my clit, rocking with his ever thrust. I loved the wet slide of his big cock in me, loved the slap of his thighs against mine when he got wound up and really went for it. I rubbed myself as he pumped into me. His hand slid around my stomach, pulled me up.

"Put your foot on the bed," he groaned. When I did, he slid in deeper, made me moan.

Then his hand came around and cupped my mound, putting pressure on my clit as he thrust into me from behind, my arm reaching back around his neck. I looked back, craned my neck for his kiss, all tongue and teeth and wild urgency. He pressed hard, made me come again. I dipped forward onto the bed, my inner muscles convulsing around his thick invasion. He gripped my hips to hold me still and thrust into me fast and hard, again and again until I felt him come, felt the hot liquid rush of his orgasm inside me. I clawed at the sheets as he finished, as if I could climb the bed.

He lay on his side and pulled me back against him to spoon me. Nothing had ever felt so good as his hot skin, his body wrapped around me, caressing me, holding me, kissing my hair.

"So beautiful," he said, "so perfect."

I couldn't say a word. It was too good. I didn't want to spoil the moment with anything I might say. Because I only wanted to ask one thing. How could my worst enemy make love to me like that? And I wasn't prepared to hear an answer for it.

He held me in his arms, nuzzled my neck and ear, whispered the sweetest things. Gathering me closer to his chest, he whispered to me.

"No matter what happens, I don't want us to lose this," he said.

"What do you mean?" I asked, suddenly less cozy and hazy, more alert.

"When the factory closes, don't let that come between us, Maggie."

"How?" I asked.

I sat up, scooted away from him on the bed. I even reached for the sheet. I couldn't believe what I was hearing, and I sure as hell couldn't hear it naked and uncovered. I felt like I'd been slapped.

"You know what I mean. I mean I like you too much, no, like isn't the word. My feelings for you are too strong to let business get in the way. This may have started out because we were on opposite sides of the factory closure, but you have to see now that we're more than that."

"The factory closure," I said flatly.

"We both know what the recommendation has to be. I'm just glad that you decided to let that go. To live in the moment and stop carrying the weight of the world," he said it so affectionately, reached out to touch my curls. I jerked away.

"I never dreamed after all we've been to each other and after what you've seen in this community that you'd still shut it down," I said in disbelief.

"What? You thought that because we were sleeping together, I'd turn in a false report? I mean, you should know that I considered it, even though it would cost me my job. That's how attracted I am to you. But in the end, I couldn't sacrifice my integrity. I came here to do a job, and to do it well. The fact that I got mixed up with you is a definite plus, but it doesn't change anything ultimately," he said.

I wanted to smack him in his smug face. I felt sick, betrayed, furious as hell.

"So you're saying I should be flattered that you decided to fuck me and fuck over the entire town at the same time? You'll probably win a plaque for multitasking. I really thought there was more to you than a shiny city boy out to make a buck. That was my mistake, not taking you at shallow face value. I thought when I met you that you were a slick piece of shit, and I should've trusted my first impression."

I scrambled out of the bed and started pulling on my clothes.

"Wait, Maggie, it came out wrong. I can explain. I'm crazy about you. I don't want this to come between us. I'm sure you think I'm the asshole right now, but I'm just the guy who makes the report. I have to call it like I see it. Hadley's the asshole shutting the place down. I just ran the numbers. And I ran into you. This amazing, smart-mouthed girl that I—"

"Just put out of business? Yeah. That's me. My daycare, all my teachers, and aides, everybody. We're just collateral damage to you. Numbers on a spreadsheet. But I'm more than that, and I could never consider being with a man who can't tell the difference between his heart and the bottom line. It comes down to integrity and values, not doing a job. And you've just shown me that you have neither of those things. I hope karma gives you exactly what you deserve."

"Maggie, wait—" he called out.

"What for? More crap about how you really like me despite having to destroy my life? Go fuck yourself," I said.

I picked up my shoes and walked out barefoot. If I was going to have to do the walk of shame, I might as well get on with it.

He flung the door open, stepped out into the hall as if to follow me.

"You're naked. Get back inside before I call the cops," I said, stomping down the stairs.

"You can't leave like this. You don't get to have a tantrum and walk out. That's ridiculous. Come sit down and we'll discuss—ow, shit! Did you just throw your shoe at me?" he said.

"Yeah, and I got another one if you don't leave me alone," I said.

I turned around and walked out. For once he did the wise thing and didn't follow me.

What the hell was I going to do? I had to face everyone I loved when they knew I'd slept with the enemy. I had to find some way to explain what I'd done, and how I'd believed something that wasn't true—that he'd come to care about me and all of us too much to hurt us that way. That I'd been wrong and arrogant and we were all screwed. No more factory, no more adjacent businesses that depended on it including mine.

I'd have to come up with a plan. When I wasn't pissed off and stomping down Oak Street in only one shoe.

16

JEREMIAH

I paced for a while, took a shower, left her a voicemail. Then I finished my report and sent it in. The recommendation was clear. The factory had to be shut down and relocated. Nothing I'd seen and no one I'd met or slept with altered the hard facts. If it was heartless, then so be it. Business was heartless, and I was very good at it. Excellent, in fact.

Tyler called in the morning to see if I was going to be back in the city by the end of the week.

"I'll be back tomorrow. I'm finishing up early."

"So, didn't go well with the feisty redhead?" he asked.

"You could say that."

"Care to elaborate?"

"No," I said.

"That bad?"

"Worse," I said grimly.

"Worse like you need a drink or ten or worse like you need stitches?" Tyler quipped.

"She did throw her shoe at me."

"Ouch. Was it a high heel?" he said, trying to stifle his laughter.

"It was a wedge, so it was heavy as hell."

"Did you put ice on your boo-boo?" he chuckled.

"No. And I don't expect you to sympathize with my woman troubles since you've sworn off of them."

"I have not sworn off women. I'm just staying off them for now. When I'm interested, I'll consider it."

"But sex was your favorite hobby," I supplied.

"I also like working out," he countered.

"You can't be serious. That's not the same thing."

"Really? You don't say?" Tyler said sarcastically. "You worry about your own issues. Like Cinderella with the shoe missile. She sounds like a keeper."

He hung up. I did not feel better. People who thought having a twin was the most comforting thing in the world had clearly never met my brother, the hardass with the smart mouth.

There was nothing for it but to take my leave and head out of town. I walked into Ron's office at the plant. I liked and respected the general manager, and I wanted to speak to him in person.

"I reckon I know what you're here for. And it's not another tour of the label licker room," he said grimly, hands in his pockets.

I saw the bald spot starting at the crown of his head, thought of the cruise he wanted to take his wife on. I was moved by this, by the years he'd given this plant, and what he'd have left when he was out of work. I didn't want that—I was struck with the force of how I wanted to stop the inevitable from happening.

"It's nothing to do with you, Ron. I think you do a fine job and run this place like it was your own. Your plant has a good safety record and all your workers speak highly of you. You have a lot to be proud of. And you understand nothing's official. I'm not the final word on this. It's just about the numbers. I'm submitting everything to Hadley, and they'll review the report and make a decision."

"So when can we expect the call?"

"I'm not sure of a timeline, but I'd say in the next couple of weeks. The jury's technically out till then regardless of my report. So you can't notify anyone of an outcome until there is one."

"So my hands are tied? I can't even tell my people that they have to look for work?"

"Not yet. I just wanted to speak to you privately because you were very gracious to me, and I believe you have a right to know what to expect," I said.

"I appreciate that, son," he said, and offered me his hand.

I shook his hand, but I didn't feel good about it. I felt dishonorable somehow, and it was uncomfortable as hell. Not as uncomfortable as my next stop would be though. I parked at the Fun Factory. A bunch of little kids were playing on the colorful plastic equipment inside the fence. I wondered how that one kid with the tantrums did with the blocks I sent, and how many of these kids would have to move and never see their friends again because I filed a report on the output and operating costs of their parents' plant. My conscience was acting up, and I didn't know what to do about it.

I went to the office and found Maggie at her desk, looking out the window at the kids playing. When I knocked on the open door, her attention snapped back, first to her computer screen, then to me. She frowned, and I could feel her disdain right through to my spine. I was the last person she wanted to see. She got to her feet, palms on her desk, and met my eyes.

"What?" she said.

"I'm leaving town."

"Good," she said. She was cool and terse, stood waiting on me to continue.

"I'm sorry that things turned out this way," I said lamely.

I wasn't sure what I had wanted to happen, maybe that she'd run into my arms and say the only thing that was important was what we'd found together, what we shared. That sure as hell wasn't on the menu. She was pissed. It was written all over her face.

She crossed her arms. I half expected her to address me sternly using my middle name. This must be her teacher pose, I thought ruefully.

"I'm sure you are. Thanks for stopping by," she said stiffly, like it was gagging her to even be polite to me.

I left without another word. If she was done with me, I'd be done with her as well.

17

MAGGIE

I hoped he hadn't seen my computer screen, my search for preschools and early childhood centers that might need an administrator or even a teacher. I was looking for a position for myself since my daycare was going to fold. I was looking to print out a list of possible places to apply for my staff, because they were family to me, and I had no intention of turning them out without a way forward. I checked the bank balance again, for the business and my personal account. I had some money saved. I would use it to give my workers a good severance. Yes, I'd probably wish I had a cushion for myself when I was out of work, but if worst came to worst, I had a house I could sell. I could go live with my parents or with Layla for a while until I found a way to start over. I was in a better position than my staff, several of whom were single moms with student loan debt. I was already drafting out a plan.

I got a call from a student's mom, saying she had seen Jeremiah at the plant. She asked if we were dating.

"I've seen him a few times but that's it. Why?" I asked.

"I wondered if he might've told you something, how it's gonna go for the plant," she said, nervousness in her voice.

"I wish I knew. Obviously we're all praying for the plant to stay open for years to come. I know he's done here and leaving town but I haven't seen his report. My guess is it doesn't look good, but you're asking a daycare worker for her opinion on corporate shutdowns," I said.

"Okay, thanks," she said, and hung up.

That day, several parents hung around at pickup time asking if we'd heard anything.

"Nothing's definite," I said, "We can always hold out hope."

"You think they'll shut down?" Kim asked me later.

"I don't know the outcome of this," I said uncomfortably. "But I'd say there isn't much chance of a happy ending here."

"That's what I thought," she said. "Do you care if I start applying for jobs?"

"I think it's the practical thing to do. If you need time off for an interview, I'll cover your shift," I said. "I'm going to tell everyone else the same. That if we find out the plant is shutting down, we'll work around schedules to make sure you get time for job hunting and these kids get cared for. You know you all mean the world to me—" I broke off.

"Don't, I'll cry," she said.

Everything pointed to crisis, to the disaster I'd dreaded. I had to make a plan and go forward. I couldn't waste time feeling sorry for myself. I fell for the wrong guy. People did it every day. It was the fact I missed him that made me hate myself. To think what he did to my family, my friends, my whole town and to miss him anyway—it was unforgivable.

I went for drinks with the girls at Cecil's one night. Not even that cheered me up.

"So, we have a bunch of people calling the Health Department wanting counseling or anxiety meds or to know when we're launching support group for people who are gonna be out of a job," Layla said, scooping up some queso.

"Well, aren't you a ray of sunshine tonight," Sarah Jo said.

"What? Her fuckboy's shutting down the plant. This place is going to hell," Layla said.

"Promise me that you never worked a suicide hotline when you were training to be a counselor," I said. "Because you managed to make me feel like a worse kind of shit than I already do."

"Why do you feel shitty? You didn't shut the plant down," Layla said. "You're not in control of the actions of others. Get yourself another drink, order a suction vibrator tonight, you'll be fine in a week."

"Do I have to pay for that advice?" I cracked with an eye roll.

"Maggie, she doesn't get it. She's a smart cookie, but she's pretty blind to love," Sarah Jo said.

"Wait, who said anything about love?" I demanded, "I liked him. He was really incredible in bed. He was also a horse's ass. The guy gave me the full-court press and then fucked us all over anyway."

"Is it definite then?" Gracie asked.

"Nothing's for sure, but I'd bet on it. I am betting on it. I'm letting workers off for interviews starting Monday. My staff needs to know they have places to go. I wish I could help more. Start like the biggest daycare on earth and hire everybody from the plant."

"Anyway, so he was incredible in bed. There were tides of passion and all that crap. You didn't catch feelings did you? Tell me Sarah Jo is wrong; tell me you know better than to catch feelings for somebody who stands for everything you hate," Layla said.

"I'm not heartbroken or anything, I just... miss him."

"You miss him?" Gracie asked. "The douche who seduced you and trashed the factory anyway?"

"I'm with Gracie, what the hell?" Layla said.

"She's in love. Give her a fucking break," Sarah Jo said, "and you two are the least romantic people I know. It's so weird that we're friends."

"I'm practical. I'm the one who can jailbreak your Fire Stick to get you free wrestling without a subscription. I also babysit your little drool-box for free," Layla said.

"People are lining up to babysit my little drool-box as you call her. She's adorable."

"Who was the lucky winner tonight?" I said.

"My in-laws. What can I say? They're great."

"You're like the poster child for happy marriages, I swear. Who would've thought after what Ryan put you through that it would all turn out so great?" Layla asked.

"Yeah, rub it in," I said, "The last chip is mine." I popped the last tortilla chip in my mouth and swigged my drink. "And just so you know. I am not in love with Jeremiah Leeds," I added, even though deep down, I knew it was a damn lie.

JEREMIAH

If I kept it up, I'd outweigh Tyler, and he was a gym rat. And when I'd told him exercise was no substitute for sex, I'd had no idea how right I was. Because working out to keep in shape was one thing. Working out because it's your only physical outlet and you're so damn frustrated and lonely is another thing. A more miserable thing. So instead of just working out four days a week, I was up to twice a day. Pull ups, pushups, ab work, circuit training. I almost went to a hot yoga class.

Tyler was the worst. He kept calling to tell me to go out with someone new, get my mind off Maggie.

"You have to get out there, man. Don't just shrivel up and die because she dumped you. Go out, get laid, you'll feel better," he insisted.

"If that's not the pot calling the kettle celibate, I don't know what is," I said, grouchy.

"See, that salty attitude is not going to get you hooked up. Next thing you know, you'll be shaking a broom at people and telling them to get off your lawn."

"I don't have a lawn. I have a townhouse. The grounds are tended by an off-site contractor," I said.

"You're so literal. You're going to turn into an old man overnight. Pining over some chick," he said. "What does Mom say?"

"She says get over it and get back to work. What else can she say? It's how she lived her life. I'm just glad she's seeing someone and getting out more, finally getting to have her own life, you know?"

"Yeah, our mom is having more sex than both of us put together," Tyler said.

"God, I wish you hadn't said that! I met the guy. And now there's this image in my head. Shit," I said.

"You know you love me. Get a woman. Quit moping," he said.

"You should not become a therapist," I said. "Just a piece of advice."

"I don't take job advice from guys who hate their work, sorry," he said. "How's it going at Hadley?"

"They gave me a bonus because I did such a thorough job on the last inspection. So you'll get a nice Christmas present," I said ruefully.

"How nice? Apple watch nice or private island nice?"

"Somewhere in between. How's work?"

"Same. It's work."

"Yeah, great talk," I joked. "Do you and your counselor just sit and stare at each other after an answer like that?"

"I'm not vibing with the counselor. I need a new one. I just didn't feel comfortable with him. Like he was judging me," he said, sounding edgy.

"So find a new one."

"I may not stay here, I don't know," he said. "I get restless."

"You need—you know what, I don't know what you need. You're the only one who knows that. Let me know what you decide, and if you need anything," I said.

"Okay," he said, and hung up.

I needed to get Maggie out of my head, but there was no way I could look at another woman, not after what we'd been to each other. It didn't feel like it was too soon or like I'd change my mind eventually. It felt like I would never have any interest in another woman. Like it was beyond imagination. I decided to do some more sit ups. Then I poured a rum and cola—the Loser's Lounge drink we'd had after the softball game-and let myself sit there and think of her.

Her riot of red curls, her cleverness and humor, the way she'd gone soft and mushy over some rabbits and goats, and the way I had felt standing with her in my arms looking out over that view by the creek. It had been a perfect moment right then. My chest ached for it, for her.

I didn't regret what I'd done. I regretted that I'd hurt Maggie with my actions. But that was a half-assed apology at best, and she deserved better than that. I could see it from her side, like the scales had fallen from my eyes. That I'd made love to her and then betrayed her in the same breath. I could not acquit myself of it, but I could try to redeem myself. Try and prove to myself, and maybe to her, that I was more than just the asshole that ruined her life.

MAGGIE

The three and four-year-olds were watching *Finding Dory* in the common room, all of us sitting on our rainbow rug. I reminded myself to keep swimming, just like the movie said. Then the door opened, and it was Ron from the plant. His kids were in high school, so they weren't in my care. It was unusual for him to stop by here.

I got to my feet and ushered him into my office, nodding to Kim to keep an eye on the kids.

"What can I do for you today?" I said.

"I've got some news, and I figured you had a right to hear it. The call came in from Hadley an hour ago. In eight weeks, we're shutting down for good."

"Oh, Ron," I said. "I'm so sorry. Is there anything I can do? Obviously, we'll stay open through the shutdown, so your workers won't have to worry about daycare too."

"Find yourself a new job like the rest of us, I suppose," he said. "I knew you were seeing that boy from Hadley. I figured if you knew anything you would've told us, so I owed you the same courtesy."

"I didn't know anything for sure," I said. "But I had the impression it wasn't good."

"So he talked to you, too?" he said.

"What do you mean?"

"Before he left town, Jeremiah stopped by my office to tell me he was putting in his report and give me the heads up that it probably wasn't going our way. He didn't want me to be blindsided by the outcome. He's a good kid. Shame about his job," Ron said, shaking his head. "But he didn't sound like he'd be at that job for very long. Way I see it, maybe this was his wake-up call. Spending time here, with you. Gives a man an idea about the kind of life he wants."

"Thank you for concern, and for letting me know. I'll let my staff know later on today."

"You have a good day now," he said, and left.

I rejoined the kids and teachers, and when the kids went down for rest time, I called the staff into the common room and told them.

"You all have been the best teachers and aides, and you have loved these kids and looked out for them and for each other. I couldn't have asked for a better work family. And this is a difficult time for us all. I'd appreciate if you all stay on for the remaining eight weeks if possible. I'll do anything in my power to help you. I'll give you a reference, make calls, get your shift covered so you can interview. In eight weeks, when the factory shuts down, our business will be done. We have no hope of remaining open and would lose money in the attempt. I've arranged for you each to get a month's severance pay in addition to your wages. And I thank you from the bottom of my heart," I said.

"You don't have that kind of money," Kim whispered to me later. "Everything you have just about is tied up in this place."

"I've got this covered," I said.

"Did you sell your car or empty your 401K?" she demanded.

"I'm young. I can save more money once I get another job. I've got some stuff printed out that I'm going to post in the kitchen tomorrow, job openings nearby that you should try for. I did a little hunting around for us."

"We want to work for you, and you know it."

"I wish we could make that happen," I told her.

Then I went in my office, torn between crying and breaking things. I felt furious and powerless and felt something like grief as well. I wanted to call Jeremiah and tell him I hated him, that I hoped he fell off a skyscraper in the city. But I knew there was no point, and even if there was, I'd cry when I heard his voice. I wanted to scream and cry and smash my computer, and I was furious most of all at myself for thinking I had the power to stop this from happening. My arrogance had gotten me exactly nothing. The factory was still shutting down. Jeremiah still chose his job over me. He still left town. We were all in the same boat here, and I had helped drill holes in it.

So I sat at my desk and composed an email to all our parents and guardians, assuring them that we'd stay open throughout the transition, and I gave the tentative date for the final day. All programs would continue except for the newer after school care program I'd begun. It would be discontinued starting next week. It wasn't turning a profit, and it didn't make sense to drain my savings for two more months just to keep four kids. A swell of sadness came over me at the fact that I'd let these people down. I tried to end on a cheerful note, but it was pretty useless. Which was exactly how I felt at the moment.

JEREMIAH

I called her. I knew I had to. The order had come down to close the processing plant, and I knew she'd know by now. I had to hear how she was taking it, even if it meant more of her yelling at me. Craven, I yearned to hear her voice. I had to make sure she was okay. So I dialed the number.

"Fun Factory, this is Maggie speaking," she said.

"Maggie, it's me," I said.

"What do you want Jeremiah?" She sounded exhausted and not at all happy to hear from me.

This wasn't going to be easy. "They told me about the order to shut the plant down. I wanted to see how you are."

"I'm exactly how you'd think I am. I'm mad as hell. I'm out of a job, just like everybody else is or will be after this is over. When the dust settles, there won't be anything left but the gas station and the grocery store the way I figure it. Everything from the dry cleaners to the flower shop depends on that factory. So you can't call me and ask me how I am after you did this. You made this happen," she burst out in one breath, her voice ferocious and tight.

"It wouldn't have mattered what I put in my report, Maggie. There's an oversight committee that would've checked the numbers, shut the place down and fired me for dereliction of duty. Would that have made you happy?" I said.

"Maybe!" she shot back. "You took *everything*."

Her voice sounded a little bit sad. I told myself it was sadness over the fate of her community, not sadness over us.

"Would you have wanted a man who compromised his integrity, who didn't go to the trouble to be honest even if it was painful? Do you think I wanted to close that place down? Those are good people, Maggie. I know those people, because of you. I know that Ron can't take his wife on a fucking cruise for their anniversary now, and I'm part of the reason for that. You made it all human for me, not just numbers. But I wasn't going to lie, give up what I know about myself, that I'm honest to a fault. That I did the right thing even when it hurt like hell. If the numbers had been there, the report would've looked different. But I didn't commit fraud and tamper with spreadsheets. But I know as loyal as you are to everyone you care for, you wouldn't have wanted me to do that to myself, to compromise my integrity and for an outcome I couldn't even promise. I'm worth more than that—and you showed me that. That I'm more. So hear my explanation or not, but know this: I didn't set out to hurt you, and I didn't go into this thinking I'd—" I broke off. "That I'd care for you the way I do. Or that at the end of the day that wouldn't matter to you at all."

"I'm really glad you're so pleased with how you conducted yourself. I hope they give you a trophy and a big ass bonus so you can buy a sports car big enough for your ego. You have a lot of nerve calling me and acting like you're the injured party here. I'm not good at being a victim, so you can have that part if you want it. I've got plans to make," she said, and hung up.

She was pissed, and she was disappointed in me, or in some idea she had where I could be the white knight who saved them all. But mainly she was hurt. I heard it in the edge of her voice, and I needed to see her. To hold her. To look in her eyes, to see if I could help in any way.

I got my stuff together and got in my car. I headed for that town in the hills where I'd left her, where I'd left so much damage behind. It was a fool's errand. She was going to shout and cuss at me. But maybe when she was done, I could hold her. I could help her see her way clear to starting something new with or without me. That was the thing. I wanted her to be okay, whether I got to be with her or not. That was new for me, concern over someone else's well-being outside my immediate family. She made me feel that, and I was following it home to her.

I called Tyler to tell him, "I'm going back to see her. They shut down the factory and she's pissed as hell."

"Then you're driving the wrong way, brother. Head the opposite direction of the woman who's pissed at you. Did you learn nothing growing up with our mom? You don't wanna ask if she's okay or if she needs anything. She'll hand you your balls on a plate and laugh at you."

"That's one thing growing up with a tough ballbuster like Mom did for me, Ty. It made me tougher. I'm not afraid to face her like a man. I want to help her through this. Even though asking for help is like the last thing she would do."

"So, mark my vote down under Terrible Idea. Good luck," he said.

He was probably right. But I was pretty sure it was the best terrible idea I'd ever had.

21

MAGGIE

What in the blistering hell was that man doing at my door?

It wasn't bad enough he showed up in my dreams every night or that I spent half my time trying not to think of him when I was working or showering or searching for jobs. It didn't matter that he'd made me laugh and made me come and made me feel safe. It mattered that he'd done all that as a lie, that he did those things while stealing our livelihood away with the other hand. I had to learn to hate him. Without the sick, sad, missing-him ache in my stomach all day, every day.

I was already hopeless and defeated and looking desperately awful.

Then he had to go and show up at my job. Not cool.

I tore the door open, surprised it didn't fly off its hinges in protest. He stood there, with the nerve to look perfect. His short dark hair was just a touch longer than it had been the last time I had my hands in it. There was a trace of stubble, just a shadow along his jaw. The rush of feelings was so unfair, the way my body heated and tried to cant toward him like some stupid plant tilting toward the sunlight. I felt tears thick in my throat and my hands tingled with the urge to touch him. Instead, I stood there waiting for some godforsaken explanation.

"Why are you here?" I demanded. "I'm working. I still have a job for the moment, and I'm shorthanded because half my staff has job interviews. I don't have time for a private meeting."

I sounded exasperated, but there was, I fancied, a hint of relief in my voice. Because the sight of him filled some need I hadn't wanted to acknowledge.

"So I take it you didn't miss me," he deadpanned, stepping in the room.

I knew I couldn't go in my office, not when I had to keep an eye on the three watching Dora the Explorer while the bigger kids played outside, and Kim watched the nappers in the toddler room.

"It'll have to be here," I said, my voice low. "Say what you came to say and then go."

"That's actually better than I expected. I expected another shoe to the face."

"You sure as hell deserve one."

"I'd like to explain," he began.

"And I'd like to rewind. This is your fault, Jeremiah. Yours alone. Everyone I know is in a panic with their livelihood in jeopardy because you didn't like the look of some numbers. We aren't numbers here, Company Man. We're people who welcomed you into our lives, were kind to you, and you repaid that by trashing the town as sure as if you'd lit a grease fire."

"Are you done? I know you hate me, and you blame me.

I know all that. What I don't know is how you are, really. Do you need my help, can I do something to make this less awful for you?"

I felt my face go red with anger. "You do not get to show up and comfort me. How dare you think I'd fall into your arms!" I said. I took a precautionary step back just in case I got overwhelmed by my damnable yearning to do just that. I turned so I could watch the kids at the carpet. It also had the benefit of partly turning my back on him.

"Tell me if you're okay."

"How could I be okay? Look at what happened! I have never been the kind of woman who wanted to be saved. But then the one time a guy comes along who could save me and a lot of other people I love, he chose not to. Jesus, Jeremiah, you broke my heart." I said it, and I wasn't sorry.

I let my guard down for just one minute, told the truth. That he had left me brokenhearted. I quit putting on the brave front for just an instant and let him see how deeply hurt I was, how I was biting my lip to keep the tears that were standing in my eyes from falling. I looked up at the ceiling and blinked them away as fast as I could. Then I met his eyes.

He reached for me then. My throat was tight with wanting him to hold me, wanting to be folded up against his chest and held by him, by the man I was stupid enough to fall for. I shook my head and backed away.

I couldn't let him touch me. If he did, I knew where that would lead. I couldn't risk it.

"Please go," I said, my voice steadier than I felt.

The brush of his hand on my sleeve as he left, the click of the door shutting behind him. That's all I was left with. It was what I said I wanted. It's what I asked him to do. So why did I want to howl and weep? Why did I want to turn and run after him? I hated myself for falling for him, for offering him my heart when I had known what he was here to do in the first place.

22

JEREMIAH

"Some things can't be forgiven, bro. Sorry to break it to you," Tyler said when I called him.

"That's not the most supportive thing you could have said," I pointed out.

"I'm just saying. I don't think it's unforgivable, but I'm not her. Everybody's different. Me, I think forgiving yourself is the hardest. That's a fucking mountain climb right there. So maybe ask yourself if she's that hurt by you, or if she just can't forgive herself."

"You're deep. It's all that therapy talking, right?" I joked.

"Yeah, I'm a regular Dalai Lama. Put in your quarter and out pops the wisdom," he said.

"I'm not sure she's going to open up about her feelings toward me or herself. She's hurt and mad and a hundred percent not okay," I said.

"Well, what'd you expect?"

"Her parents won't rent me a room. It's like I'm blacklisted. I had to go get a hotel room in the next town over. And that's worse because not only do I have to stay in another town, it's right across from the restaurant where I took her for dinner."

"The one where you were making out on the sidewalk and they literally asked you to come inside and get a room? That was epic," he said with a laugh.

"They actually gave us a room, a private dining room. To eat in."

"Come on. Don't tell me you didn't have sex there."

"We didn't have sex there. I was tempted, beyond anything you can imagine, but I wasn't going to do that there. Not in a public place, not when it was our first time together."

"If you didn't want me to give you any shit, why'd you even call me in the first place? You want tough love, call Mom. You want some ball-busting, call me."

"Yeah, I must've forgotten. Listen," I said. "This whole mess got me thinking. I want to make some changes. I haven't been happy with my job for a while. It's altered my career trajectory and—"

"Sorry, nodded off there. When you talk about your career and your business degree and shit, I get bored."

"I'm serious, I have some decisions to make."

"So go make them," Tyler said.

For the one of us who'd been through therapy, he sure didn't have much patience for talking things out. He was more a man of action.

"It was good talking to you," I said, and I meant it. In a lot of ways, Tyler understood me better than anyone.

"It helps to hear your voice," he said, "even when I'm busting your balls. It feels good to be normal. That you don't talk to me like I'm a bomb that's about to go off."

"Well, I've known you all our lives. You've always been like that, so why would I be skittish now?" I joked.

"Thanks," he said, and I knew he was sincere.

I knew he was rudderless since he'd left the Marines; that he didn't have any direction. I wanted to help with that. I wanted to step up and be there for my brother. And I wanted to get Maggie back, which was priority one. There were only a handful of people in my life I really loved, and I'd do anything for them. It was something that made Maggie and me alike—she just cared about her whole community and had a sense of family with them that I didn't have. So it would piss her off to admit it, but we'd both go to the wall for love. I was about to prove it.

I just had to drive out west of town and turn north when I saw the goats. I had some farmers to talk with.

23

MAGGIE

I was dragging my feet when I showed up at the B&B to help out at the front desk while my mom caught up on the bookkeeping. She took one look at me and reached into the little fridge behind the counter and handed me a Diet Coke. I cracked it open gratefully.

"Got anything stronger?" I joked.

"I've got a couple White Claws in there. For when it's slow," she said.

My eyebrows shot up, "You drink on the job?" I said.

"No, I'm kidding. But look at you."

"Yeah, I look like I feel. Like I've had my ass kicked by life in general."

"You're looking out for everyone but yourself," she said with a *tsk* sound.

"I have to take care of my staff. They threw their lot in with me when I was so young I barely qualified for a loan, and they believed we could make a go of it. And we did."

"Yes. And we're so proud of all you've done. How's the job hunt?"

"Dismal. There are no childcare positions in driving

distance that would be anywhere close to what I was earning with the Fun Factory. I don't want to move away, so I'm looking into taking some classes back at the community college."

"Oh really? What kind of classes?" she said.

"I could get my LPN and get a job at the hospital. Hospitals are recession-proof and the benefits there are great. Layla thought I could even get on at the Health Department with just my CNA while I'm finishing up my LPN course work."

"That's great," she said flatly, "Except you hate needles."

"Well I won't be getting shots, I'd be giving them. It's not my first choice. I mean—I like to run things. But unless I want to manage a freaking Ann Taylor Loft in Pendleton for ten bucks an hour, I better get over it."

"You could never work at Loft," my mom said. "I've seen your closet. They don't let the staff wear Pete the Cat t-shirts."

"Nice, Mom. Real supportive," I said, rolling my eyes.

"Hey, I turned away your Hadley drone when he wanted to stay here again."

"He came here?"

"Yes. I sent him on his way with an earful about how he treated my daughter."

"Oh, God. Mom. You didn't."

"Of course, I did," she said proudly. "Who do you think taught you how to give people a piece of your mind? Not your father, that's for sure. That man would eat soup with a fly in it before he'd send it back. I let that boy know exactly what I thought of the way he does business. Seducing an innocent young girl like my daughter—"

"Mom, you realize I'm not Sleeping Beauty, right?"

"I can pretend you're totally innocent if I want to. It's a mother's privilege," she said sarcastically.

"What did he say?" I said.

"You really care?"

"No. I just wondered if you made him cry or wet his pants or anything like that one time in Kohl's when you got that assistant manager to apologize and he just put his nametag down and walked out?"

"That was an exciting day. And if they'd just honored my coupon it wouldn't have been an issue. Anyway, your young man held his own."

"He isn't mine."

"I think you may be mistaken in that," my mother said archly.

"What are you talking about?"

"He was respectful and said he understood why we couldn't accommodate him, but he didn't grovel or act tragic."

"Didn't you want him to? I mean, you did it to humiliate him."

"No, I did it to get my message across. My daughter is worth more than he could ever fathom," she said. I admit, that made me smile. "I liked his response."

"Which was?" I prompted.

"He said, 'If I were you, I'd be pissed at me too.' It showed empathy without being a suck up. You and I both know that only the strong would survive a relationship with you. You're a force of nature, and you always have been. You don't need someone who'll kiss your ass, Maggie. You need a man who can stand on his own two feet and back you up when things get hard. And one who will challenge you when you're being too stubborn for your own good."

"I don't need a man," I said, showcasing just how stubborn I could be.

"You might want to hear him out," she said.

"Why would I want to do that? To give him one more chance to disappoint me?"

"To find out what he's made of, honey. Because this is going to piss you off, but I think you two are a lot alike."

"I do not go around—"

"Aaand you proved my point," she laughed. "Of course you haven't made the same choices he has. But you both take no prisoners and you have a heart of gold."

"Since when does Company Man have a heart at all, much less one of gold?" I demanded.

"You should discuss that with him," she said. "It was slow this afternoon, so I caught up on the books then. I'll cover the desk if you want to go find him."

"Mom, it was slow because of the economic crash we have coming. You can't afford to be turning away guests like you did with him."

"You let me worry about that, and you take care of your own mess," she warned. I hugged her.

"Thanks, Mom.

Then I stood on the sidewalk trying to decide what to do. I decided to brazen it out. If I'd learned anything in my adult life, it was that my mom was almost always right. She didn't make my decisions for me, not even when I was four and insisted on wearing cowboy boots everywhere—but part of maturity was learning to listen to the people who always have my best interests at heart. My mom. Layla and Sarah Jo. So I dialed his number.

"Hello?" he said.

"It's Maggie," I said.

"I know. I mean, I'm glad you called. What can I do for

you?" He asked. He sounded awkward. It was annoyingly adorable on someone so masculine and self-assured.

I couldn't pretend I didn't feel a rush of excitement sweep along my skin at just the sound of his voice. I was done pretending. If I wanted something real, I had to be willing to face it and untangle the mess we'd made. That started with something I wasn't particularly good at. Listening.

24

JEREMIAH

"I've reconsidered hearing you out. Would you like to meet somewhere?"

"Yes. Absolutely. I'm staying in Pendleton, but I can meet you wherever you want." I said.

"I'll meet you at the coffee shop on Magnolia Street. About an hour?"

"I'll be there."

"Good," she said.

She was fifteen minutes early, but I was already waiting in a booth.

"You're early," she said, sitting across from me.

"I didn't want you to show up and have to wait on me and change your mind."

"I don't want to have this conversation," she confessed. "But I know it's the right thing to do. No matter how uncomfortable I am."

"I'm not trying to make you uncomfortable. I appreciate you hearing me out."

We ordered coffee and sat in silence for a minute.

"I'll try to keep an open mind," she said.

"Good. I want you to see here, on my phone, these are the numbers and that in green in the column beside them is the acceptable range for those numbers."

"Wait, what?" she said.

"They're listed for reference so you can see that the plant simply didn't have the productivity and cost-efficiency to continue."

"I know what they mean. I just can't believe I put on a cute top and swallowed my pride so you could show me a fucking spreadsheet, Jeremiah. Is that all you've got?" she asked.

"I did what was necessary, and it was the right thing. I didn't come to apologize for my decision, but to tell you I was sorry for hurting you and to see how you are."

"I'm mostly pissed off right now," she said.

"I can see that."

"What did you say to my mom?"

"What?" I said.

"At the B&B. What did you say to her?"

"Not much. She wouldn't rent me a room and let me know exactly why. She also described you as her sweet and innocent daughter," I gave a smirk.

"You made an impression on her and I was curious how you did it."

I faltered. "I just told her I'm looking into making some changes."

"To your green column of acceptable range?" she snapped.

"No. In a number of areas, actually."

"Showing me your Excel worksheet didn't exactly get me to throw my panties at you," she said, "what's the rest of your defense?"

"That if I had known it would be the last time, I would

have that I would've kept you up all night exploring every inch of you curves," I admitted.

I had replayed that night in my head a hundred times or more. I wished I'd held her in my arms kissed her lips more, made sure she looked in my eyes as she came.

"Your big vindicating argument is you would've fucked me longer? Gotta say, you're not impressing me here," she had a warning note in her voice.

I decided to change tactics. "Talk to me. How are the kids? Is your staff staying on?"

"They're job hunting and going to interviews. The kids don't really get what's going on, except a few of the four-year-olds. But they're mostly excited because they think their parents will stay home all day to play with them," she sighed, sounding tired.

"You're exhausted, and you're worried about everyone but yourself," I observed.

"Oh, trust me, I'm worried about myself too," she said, voice edgy. "Like the fact that there are no daycare centers in need of an administrator or lead teacher, and the jobs that are open don't pay worth a crap. Unless I want to move two hours away from my family and friends, I'm going to have to change my career path. So, maybe as you say, changes are in order. Unwelcome changes."

She took a drink of her coffee, grimaced, and I handed her a sugar packet. She emptied it into the cup and stirred it around.

I met her eyes, and it was a long look full of meaning. She was hurt, angry at me, but the want was still there. Lust, if not the something more I hoped for. I could work with lust. I reached over and took her hand in mine and lifted it to my mouth. I kissed the inside of her wrist, the sensitive skin there. I felt her pulse leap. She drew back, but I knew she'd felt the same sizzle I had.

"How's life in the city? Closing factories and taking names?" she said wryly.

"More like working out, going to meetings, talking to my brother. He's building homes for vets now with a nonprofit. It's a temporary job. He hasn't found his place yet," I said.

"Who has?"

"I've been someplace a few times that I'd like to stay."

"Oh yeah? Where?" she asked.

"Nothing in my life has ever felt the way I did when I was with you, Maggie," I ventured.

"Just because it felt good doesn't mean it was the right thing," she said, "what I'm thinking now is you may have ruined me."

"For other men, I hope," I said archly, keeping it light enough to stay out of deep waters.

"No one has ever touched me the way you did. I'm not sure anyone can," her voice was soft.

"It would be a shame to miss that for the rest of your life. When I'm right here."

"Well, I guess I could just drift from man to man, trying out their skills, ranking them on, shall we say a spreadsheet? I'd need to assign an acceptable green value to one column," she said sarcastically.

I was clenching my fists. Even though she was just trying to goad me, I had grown hot with jealousy. I wanted to vault across the table at her and start kissing her neck, unbutton her jeans and remind her whose she was. She enjoyed watching me squirm like that, unable to hide my primal urge to claim her, to end the conversation by blowing that scale away.

"Are you interested in what your score would be on that scale?" she asked.

"If you want to tell me," I said noncommittally.

"Or do you think that some things go beyond simple numbers? That what's on a spreadsheet can't tell the whole story?"

"Clever girl, but I can't hop in a time machine, go back and force Hadley to keep the plant open. You made your point, but it's nothing more than a talking point," I said, partly irritated, partly relieved we weren't talking about her future sex partners.

"So would you say that it made you angry when I talked about quantifying something that you considered sacred?" she challenged.

"Yes," I said readily. "It did."

"Did you want to slap me?" she teased.

"That isn't what I wanted to do to you, and you know it."

I was hard for her. I had already wanted her but sparring with her this way turned me on so much.

"Oh really? So what did you want to do?" she purred.

"Several options," I said through gritted teeth, "all of them involved you naked beneath me."

"Do you remember asking me back to your room that first night?" she said.

"Of course I do. You refused."

"Ask me again," she said.

"If you're setting me up just to turn me down, I'm probably going to flip a table," I said, not entirely joking. I was so on edge.

"Would I do that to you?"

"You'd poison my coffee if you could get away with it. I'm not under any illusions that you've forgiven me."

"What if we put that aside for tonight?" she said.

"Hate sex? Because I don't hate you."

"Not hate sex. Call it bonus night. One last time. Like you said. You'd do things differently. Maybe I would too." Her voice was a siren's low, sexy whisper. I felt it like a lick along my spine.

"Why would you want to do that?" I said, trying to get my brain to work.

"I want you, Jeremiah. I've hated myself for weeks, because I shouldn't want you. Not after what you did. But does it have to matter? Does it have to be unforgivable?"

"You tell me."

"Take me to your room, Company Man," she said.

I wasn't a man who could say no to that, wasn't a man who could deny her anything. Especially not what I wanted most.

She followed me to the hotel, stepped into the elevator with me. I couldn't help the cliché elevator kiss that happened. We had the plush elevator car to ourselves, and I backed her up to the wall, slid my hands up her sides, crushing the fabric of her silky green top as I worked my tongue in her mouth. She melted for me, moved with me, licked me right back. My match in every way.

In my room, I barely got the door shut before I turned to her and kissed her again and again, softly, leisurely, giving her the tender, wet kiss like she liked.

"You are going to melt my panties right off," she said, "And you know I couldn't have hate sex. I like you. I just never wanted to admit it."

"There was never a time I didn't like you, not even when you were giving me hell at check-in," I said, "You were irritating, but in the sexiest most challenging way possible. I couldn't stay away. I still can't. Don't do this if it's just a bonus night, Maggie. You know I don't want you just one more time. Just to say goodbye. I want you back. If we can't be the way we were—"

"I don't think that's possible. Not knowing what I know now. That you can put aside liking me or caring about me or whatever you call it and destroy something so important."

I took a step back. The last thing I wanted to do was stop kissing her, but I wasn't the kind of guy who could screw first and ask questions later. I had too much respect for us both. So I pulled her over to the couch by the window and sat down.

"Talk to me. I told you I want to help you. I meant it. What can I do?"

"You can hold me. You can make love to me. Let me escape for that long," she said. Her eyes were bright. I kissed her cheek.

"If you just want to be held, I'll hold you all night," I said. "I don't expect anything from you."

"Jeremiah," she said.

When she said my name, it undid me somehow. It clawed at my chest, made me want to crush her against me, plunder her mouth, act like some damn Viking marauder. I took her hand and kissed it.

"Yes. Whatever you need, it's a yes," I said, my voice low.

"Ask me to stay the night."

"Stay the night with me, Maggie. Nothing would make me happier."

"Okay," she said with a shaky smile.

If comfort was what she needed, I could give it to her. I was willing to give her anything in my power to give. I wanted to heal her, and I'd be damn lucky if she gave me the chance. I swept her red hair back from her face and kissed her, pressing my lips to hers, softly nipping at her lips. She responded, her hands on my face. She climbed into my lap. I gathered her greedily in my arms, kissed her lips. Had her skin always been so satiny smooth? Had I missed her this much? It felt like life flowing back into my body, just holding her, touching her again. She leaned back and removed my shirt. I held her against my chest, kissed her hair. Her mouth was on my neck, kissing and sucking, making my whole body tense as nerve endings sparked and I clenched my jaw.

Maggie paused, threw her arms around my neck and hugged me. I wrapped my arms around her in a massive bear hug. It felt like that hug was putting the pieces of me back together, shards I hadn't realized were dislodged by everything that had been going on. It was possible that I needed her just as much as I wanted her.

"Why can't I stop missing you?" she whispered, "not just sleeping with you. Everything about you."

"I know," I said, holding her tight, "I can't stop thinking about you. About the way you made me laugh at the potluck, and the day we went on the picnic by the creek, how perfect that felt. It's like the lights went out or the curtain fell. As soon as I left here, left you."

"I hate that you left and that I told you to leave. I hate all of this, Jeremiah. You can't imagine how wrong every-thing's gone. I'll figure things out, and I'll be fine. I always am. But I can't put things back together. Like us. Can that be fixed?"

"It can if you'll let it. If you can move forward with me, then it will just be that one time we broke up and it damn near killed us both. You have to trust me," I said against the springy mass of curls.

"I want to," she said, "Or I want to forget. At least make me forget for tonight."

"I'll make you forget anytime you want me to," I said with a wicked grin.

I loosened my hold on her, lifted her thick, silky hair to the side and kissed her neck. Using a deep core of self-control, I savored her neck with decadent kisses that made her gasp and grab my wrist and hold it. I loved that, the way she gripped my arm to hold me there, to keep me right where she wanted me. Right where I wanted to be. The cool fabric of her top felt good against my bare chest, but I wanted her skin on skin. I drew back, watched her pout briefly until I peeled off her shirt.

"It's a pretty thing, but it was in my way. And not as pretty as these," I said, caressing the swell of her breasts teasingly above the lace of her bra. I watched goose bumps rise on her skin, the shadow of her nipples beading at my touch.

I gathered her in my arms and carried her to the bed. I lay her on top of the covers, peeled back the sheets so she could slide between them. I shucked off the rest of my clothes and climbed into the crisp, cool sheets with her. There was something lush about getting under the covers with her, being fully in bed with her, unhurried and antici-pating great pleasure. I stroked her face and kissed her lips.

"I'm so glad you're here," I said.

"I missed you so much," she said. I nodded and kissed her cheek, her forehead, her eyelids so tenderly. A tear slid out the corner of her eye. I swept it away with my thumb.

"Don't cry," I whispered against her lip., "I'm here. I have you."

"It isn't that. I don't know what it is, except the way you touch me."

"I haven't hurt you have I?" I said, pulling away from her.

"No, no, nothing like that. You're just... I don't know, it sounds weird to say it."

"When have you ever been afraid to be weird around me?" I teased and got a soft laugh from her that felt like a victory.

"You're so gentle it made me ache, okay? See? Weird."

"Beautiful," I said, and kissed her again.

I took my time kissing my way down her body, sliding down the zipper of her jeans and easing them off of her, leaving her in peach lace panties that I wanted to rip off and crush in my hands, bury my face in them and inhale. Instead I put my mouth to her through the lace, kissing, lapping until she opened her thighs for me, ran her hands through my hair, urging me on. I hooked a finger in the panties and drew them aside so I could taste her, so I could worry her sensitive bud until she was breathing so hard I could hear it, could feel the tug of building pleasure in my own body from her eager response. Too soon, her cries rang out as she pulsed against me and came apart.

I crawled up the bed and gathered her to my chest. I caressed her arm, her back, her hair. She blinked up at me, petted and adored, pink with pleasure. I kissed her forehead, "So beautiful," I said.

She nestled into me and hugged me back. Her arms sliding around my back and the way her head fitted into the hollow of my neck felt better than anything in my life. She belonged right there in my arms, like I had been formed to hold her this way and she was made to fit there. It was a wild mix of perfect peace and sharp arousal that made awareness brighter.

"Stay with me," I said, because I couldn't stop myself.

"Yes," she said, her voice muffled in the crook of my neck.

Maggie started kissing my neck, and all that sense of peace burned away. My skin was alight, my body on fire. I rolled her onto her back and kissed her, a deep, passionate kiss that could leave no doubt what I meant to do. She was moving against me all the time, hand curling behind my head, leg hooking over mine, sinuous and fiery.

"You're all mine," I told her as my hand skated down the curve of her belly to cup her between her legs, to feel the heat and slickness there.

Shameless, she arched into my touch, urging my fingers, wanting them inside her.

"Naughty girl," I grinned against her lips, "don't you want all of me?"

"Yes. I want all of you—filling me," she said.

I spread her thighs with my hand and guided my aching, rigid cock to her slit. I rubbed it back and forth, getting the head of my cock slick with her wetness, gritting my teeth against the gorgeous sensation of rubbing through her slippery arousal. My heart pounded and my vision went bright already.

"Are you ready?" I ground out.

As her answer, she grabbed my face with both hands and kissed me, her tongue in my mouth doing lewd things that sent a wave of heat down my body. She bit my lower lip softly, "Now. Please," she said. I growled in response.

I settled into the cradle of her thighs and fed my hard cock into her an inch at a time, going slow, taking all control. I wanted to give it to her hard, to feel that sweet pressure and the shock of her body around me, but I held back. I remembered distantly something about getting carried away the last time, about wishing I'd been more tender and romantic with her. Mainly I felt that hollow core of her absence filling up as I let go and sheathed myself in her fully. She gave a cry, clutched my shoulders. I held myself up with my arms on either side of her face, so we were eye to eye.

I worked her with my cock, with the rhythm and the way I moved, the stir of my shaft against her inner walls, those wetly clinging lips that I hated to withdraw from even to thrust. Soon I was hitting that place inside her that made her writhe and squirm. I kissed her, but it was uneven, messy, because I was getting close, was thrusting into her. She wrapped her arms around me, flung her leg around my hips and met my thrusts. Every time I hit the spot inside her just right, her inner muscles fluttered around me and I shivered, trying to hold off.

"Yes," I said through gritted teeth. "I know what you want. Take it."

I slid out of her almost completely and thrust back in at the angle I knew she needed. She arched off the bed, bucking and crying my name. "Jeremiah! Oh!"

It may have been the force of her coming around my cock or the shock of hearing my name on her lips at such a moment, but I came then, like lightening up my spine, shaking as if in the grip of something merciless. I pumped into her, giving her every drop, every inch of me. I felt split apart and thunderstruck.

I sat back, shaken, but she scrambled up to her knees and wrapped her arms around me and held on. She kissed my cheek, stroked my sweaty hair as if to comfort me from the most insane orgasm of my life. As if she could sense that what I needed most was contact with her, our bodies together. I got my arms around her and pressed her against me, against my heart. My breath was ragged, and she clung to me. It was a long time before I came back to myself and could speak. I lay down on a pillow and beckoned her to join me.

"You were wonderful," I said. "You always are. Even when you're angry, you're wonderful."

I don't know if it's the amazing sex talking or what, but I feel closer to you. I feel like—like I could forgive you," she said softly.

I felt my brow furrow in spite of myself. I willed myself not to say anything. But there it was. I couldn't stop myself.

"I didn't ask forgiveness. I hate that you were hurt by my actions, but if I had it to do over, even though I'd take the time to explain it all first, I wouldn't change what I did about the report. So you don't have to forgive me. You just have to be able to look at it as an unfortunate thing that happened, and we broke up over it once. But we put it aside because it wasn't the most important thing," I insisted.

Maggie propped herself up on her elbow and narrowed her eyes.

"Are you fucking kidding me?" she said.

25

MAGGIE

He didn't need to be forgiven?

"You put half the people in town out of work directly and most of the rest of us out of work by extension. You don't see anything there that's, I don't know, damaging and willfully cruel? You don't think that's a slap in the face and a long-term blow to our economy and way of life? I'm going to have to go to nursing school, for fuck's sake! I don't like sick people and I'm going to suck at it, but that's all there is left for me here!" I said, sitting up and waving my arms for emphasis.

He looked startled, taken aback. I think a little irritated, like I was being a buzz kill. But, hey, shit happens including the shit he brought down on my head when he filed that report on the factory.

"I cannot believe you can sit there, so self-satisfied, and say you don't need to ask me to forgive you. I knew you were arrogant, but this is next level. I should have known. Instead, I chose to go to bed with you because I wanted to, because I believed what I wanted to. And you're damn good at what you do. You were really convincing at playing someone who cares about me. You probably even believe it---I'm willing to bet you do. But I know what's true. You wrecked me, and it's because I invited you to. Ever since you walked into the B&B I've acted like a complete fool for you. It's past time for that to be over. So, I'm done. You did exactly what I needed you to do which is prove that you were wasting my time."

I started to drag on clothes.

"Maggie, hear me out."

"I did," I said.

"It's a miscommunication. I do apologize for hurting you. I'm very sorry for that. But I'm also mad as hell that you think this of me, that I pretended to feel something for you just to get you in bed. I came back for you because it was killing me to think of you so hurt, and I wanted nothing more than to hold you and do whatever I can to help. Let me help you and be here for you. I want that more than anything. If you need me to ask forgiveness for doing my job, I will. Don't leave. Stay and fight for what we have. You can scream and throw your shoes and call me names. Just don't walk out," he said.

I wanted to believe him, God help me, but I was so furious I wanted to rip the walls down on his head. I couldn't look at him one more minute. My heart was hardened to him, bitterness cooling my blood.

"Go to hell, Jeremiah," I said, and shouldered my purse.

I had a shower to take and a life to rebuild. I wasn't wasting another minute on a man who wasn't even sorry for trashing my life. He left half my community out of work. That wasn't a small thing, a mistake that could be overlooked. He might as well have poured out kerosene and lit a match to the plant.

I sped home, showered in the hottest water I could stand and called Layla.

"Yeah, he's a complete asshole. Coming back here with his bullshit feelings and his no apology. He isn't sorry! Can you believe he isn't fucking sorry for destroying the lives of hundreds of people?"

"Yeah, but I'm a counselor. I hear all kinds of stupid shit people say justify to themselves. It's pretty common. Assholes are a dime a dozen. I'm sorry he turned out to be a prick. Get out a bottle of wine and your vibrator and—"

"I don't need to. I slept with him. I'm so disgusted with myself."

"Don't be. No shame. If he's the asshole, that's on him. You're in love. Don't be so hard on yourself," she said.

"I am not in love."

"Yeah, and I'm a natural blonde, Mags. For real. You love the shit out of him whether you like it or not."

"I do not. If I did, I'd just have to get over it, because he's a heartless piece of crap and I hate him."

"We're back to hate now? Okay, call me when you're in the weeping stage," she said. "I'm going back to sleep."

"There is no weeping stage. There is only rage and fury and rebuilding my life. I wish I could figure out how to keep the daycare open and like, employ more people. Some other business venture or, attract another factory... I don't know."

"Go to sleep. Save the world tomorrow. Right now, you're a little hyper from the drama. Eat some sugar, get some rest," she said. "Sugar's good for panic."

"I'm not panicked," I said.

"I'm pretty sure you are. Love you, babe."

She hung up. Shit. I was not in love with him. I refuse to be in love with him, selfish fucker. *Expects me to let bygones be bygones while hundreds of people are gonna be out panhandling if they don't move far away for a job. An entire way of life, gone. Because of him. Son of a bitch.*

I rage cleaned my entire closet, made a donation pile of clothes and shoes I hardly ever wore, cussed to myself the entire time about Jeremiah Leeds. I finally fell asleep around five in the morning and slept till ten. I only woke up then because my mom called.

"Did you hear him out?"

"Yeah. It was a long, detailed explanation that just proves what an asshole he is. I tried, and I wanted to believe him, but I'm not stupid. He only cares about himself and his job. He made his choice, and I've made mine. I'm not seeing him again. If he comes to the inn, you have my permission to pepper spray him till he leaves."

"I don't have pepper spray. You know I keep a Glock."

"Mom, I love you. Please don't shoot anyone. I emptied my 401K to pay my staff a severance, so I don't have bail money," I said with a laugh.

"I'm not shooting anybody. I'm disappointed in him. Because if you're this angry, he can't be the man I thought he was. I love you, baby. And I'll make you a pie later."

"Thank you."

I flopped back down on the bed and slept for a while. Even in my dreams I was furious, hot murderous rage coursing through me. Rage was good. It could fuel my new beginning; help me solve all these problems.

26

JEREMIAH

I learned something from taking Maggie to bed and watching her walk out. I loved her. And I'd never been in love like this before. So I had to tell her, before I left. Not the sweeping, romantic scene I had pictured. Not the way I planned. But she deserved to know, and it was my last gambit, the only chance I had left to win her back, to prove what she meant to me.

I used the hotel's business center to print out the plans, to distill my entire project, into seven pages stapled together. It had to be enough. I talked to the bank, talked to the people I was moving into place to work on the project.

Then I drove to the Fun Factory, that soon-to-be-closed business she'd started all on her own and made a success. I parked and went to the door.

A blonde with a ponytail answered.

"She's not going to talk to you," she said balefully.

"You must be Kim," I said. "Please. I have something to tell her that she needs to know."

"Is it that you've found a way to save the factory?" she challenged.

"No," I said.

"Then you should leave."

She shut the door on me. I decided to come back later. At closing time, I drove up again and texted Maggie.

I'm in the parking lot. Come for a drive with me. Please.

I waited. I waited for expletive-filled texts full of emoji's giving me the finger. I waited for a simple 'hell no.' I waited, knowing she said she never wanted to see me again. Half an hour later, she came out of the building and walked straight to my car.

"You shouldn't be here."

"Please come for a drive with me. It won't take an hour. I'll bring you right back here. There's something I need to show you," I said.

"I don't want to go anywhere with you," she said. She was so calm, so matter of fact that it chilled me.

"If you come with me now, I promise after that I will leave you alone if that's what you want," I said. I was betting on myself, on my ability to convince her of how I felt. If I failed, I would lose her forever. A knot in my chest warned me I'd better give it all I had. She was worth it, worth everything.

"Fine. I'm texting my mom to let her know I'll be an hour late to cover the front desk at the inn. One hour. Then you leave me alone forever," she said.

"If that's what you want, I'll respect that," I said gravely, hiding my surge of triumph that she was willing to listen.

Maggie climbed into the passenger seat, and I cut my eyes at her. "I love your shirt. Eric Carle?"

"Very Hungry Caterpillar is a huge hit with these kids," she said flatly, not looking at me. She would be civil, but she wasn't going to make it easy. She wasn't going to let me hold her hand and profess my feelings.

I drove out west and then north of town. She finally looked at me, confusion in her eyes. I parked and took a blanket and wine out of my trunk. I spread the blanket in the spot where we'd picnicked before. On the hill overlooking the creek. I motioned to her and she sat down on the blanket, facing the sunset. It was a ferocious red-orange melting into gold, the sky above us growing a pearly violet. I opened the wine and poured two glasses. She took a sip.

"Do you like it?" I said.

"It's good," she said.

"It's very similar to what I'm looking for us to produce," I said. "It's early days, but I have the plans for you to look at. Along with my resignation letter from Hadley and the preliminary breakdown on how many local workers I expect to employ."

"What are you talking about?" she said, her brow knit in confusion.

I handed her the printout. She looked it over, read every word of the letter to Hadley in which I quit my job in protest over their callous business practices and willful outsourcing of American jobs being stolen from good, hard-working people like those of this town in the name of profit. I included a copy of the op-ed I sent in to the Washington Post about my part in the shameful practice of closing American factories to exploit low-wage foreign workers and destroy prosperous communities like this one. I had penciled in the date it was set to run in the paper nation-wide. She flipped the page and saw the drawing, the initial blueprints.

"It's a winery. I'm planning on a vineyard, a winery that gives tours and has a tasting room for events. A farm to table restaurant with a lot of the produce grown on-site and a full-service resort and spa. The initial figures show us being able to employ every worker from that factory and at least thirty more besides. That right there, in the back where the land is graded more level is where the playground will be. For the employee daycare I'm building."

"How are you doing all this?" she said in disbelief.

"I told you. I'm a good project manager. I have amassed a great deal of money and I'm financing the rest. This is going to be incredibly successful. I hired away Hadley's PR director and a friend of mine in marketing to manage our soft open and grand opening and to help with creating a brand profile and getting us media coverage. We're about to make this town a travel destination. By we, I mean the two of us, if you'll join me."

"You're building a daycare for me to run, and you're hiring every single person from that factory?" she said.

"Ron's going to be my general manager for the bottling factory. Trust me, he'll be able to afford that cruise, or one to the Greek Isles if he prefers. We'll have plenty of wine labels for the label lickers to affix, and lots of work in the fields and warehouse and resort for anyone who wants a job. The only thing I need is for the property owner to agree."

"You haven't even got the land? How are you going to do this?"

"Because you own the land, Maggie. All of this is yours. You can make this happen or shut down the whole project. You have the control."

"Why are you doing this?"

"Because I was wrong, and because I'd do anything for you. Some girls would want a Tiffany ring. What you needed from me was a business, a new heart for this community. It's going to be a hell of a place, Maggie. We'll have the place up and running in time for next year's harvest, and I've already got HGTV buying an option on a three-episode reality show of our grand opening with a tour of the facilities and enough viewership to keep us booked up and sold out for months. We'll have artisan gift shops with local products, expand as we need to. I have contacts in the hospitality and marketing industries that basically guarantee our success. We're going to bring so much tourism to this area that the local economy will never be the same. Will you do this with me?"

She stared at me, drained her wine glass, speechless.

"This is my dream now, to do this with you. To build something worthwhile and amazing, to bring jobs to this area and reinvigorate it. To be with you," I said.

"I—I guess I'll have to give you another chance then," she said with a nervous laugh. "I can't believe all this."

"I don't want a chance, Maggie," I said, "I want a wife."

I took out the ring and offered it to her. She looked at me with tears in her eyes, "Yes!" she said.

I pulled her into my lap and kissed her. She wrapped her arms around my neck and let me hold her. I felt a head rush like I'd just gone down the steepest hill of a roller coaster, a flood of pure happiness. Everything I'd ever wanted in my arms.

"I love you," I said, "I've loved you since the minute you told me we were never going to kiss again. I felt like my lungs quit working. I was sure I'd die if it were true. If I didn't' get to kiss you every day for the rest of our lives. I knew right then that I'd do anything I could to try to deserve you, to be worthy of being your husband one day."

"I love you too," she said, laughing in spite of her tears. "I've wanted to tell you for so long, but I wouldn't let myself admit it."

I made love to her there and then, on the blanket on our ground where we would build our dream. I kissed her passionately, my hands twined in her red curls that spilled across the blue blanket beneath her, used every stroke to bring her spiraling closer to ecstasy until I made her come right there on the spot where we'd build our home.

"Welcome home, my love," I said to her as I held her afterward.

EPILOGUE

MAGGIE - TWO YEARS LATER

"Danny, come back here!" I called, racing across the gardens to catch our little boy.

Whoever said one-year-olds barely toddle around never met our son. He was as fierce and determined as his daddy, and he ran everywhere. I caught up to him before he could rip up any of the vegetables in the kitchen garden outside the restaurant. The restaurant that was closed for a private party that night. His birthday.

Purple balloons decorated the dining room as I carried him inside, windblown, red-cheeked and happy.

"Come sit down, wild man," I teased him, and settled him in the highchair decorated with crepe paper in front of the sign that read "Happy Birthday Danny!" that the employees had made for him. He was a huge favorite at the restaurant with his sunny smiles and silly giggled.

Jeremiah was at my side with a glass of wine, a light, sweet white from our first harvest last year. I sipped it gratefully as he brought out the smash cake for Danny. My mom took pictures while my dad videoed the whole messy proceedings.

"Can you believe it's only been two years?" he asked. "Since the night you said you'd marry me?"

"It seems like it was just last week," I said, leaning into his shoulder as his arm looped around me. "It's been a whirlwind. And we're booked solid for the next seven months!"

"Yeah, there's no slowing down. Tyler says the barn will be done any day and we've already got weddings booked for the fall there."

"Sarah Jo has outdone herself landscaping for that. It's like a fairyland," I said.

"It's perfect, but the most perfect thing here is this," Jeremiah said, kissing my lips. "Us, and that little boy. I never dreamed I could have anything like this."

"Your mom seems to like the wine," I said. His mom was taking pictures with her phone while Danny smeared cake on his head, but she wasn't putting down her glass of pinot grigio to do it.

"She's a fan. Mainly of you, and the spa. She told me yesterday she wants massages from Jorge to be her Christmas present. Just a week of twice a day massages," he laughed.

"I think we did well, Company Man," I said with a smile.

"I think this is the best, my wife," he said and kissed me full on the mouth no matter who was looking.

"It's almost the best," I said. "The best will be when we have a christening in that beautiful, rustic event barn eight months from now."

"What?"

"I'm pregnant. It was bound to happen, the way we can't keep our hands off each other," I giggled with joy.

But his face turned serious, handsome and grave. "I love

you so much, Maggie. How do you always surprise me, always make me love you even more? Just when I'm thinking I'm the luckiest bastard on earth and there's not another thing I could wish for, you give me this. Thank you."

"I remember you had a role in this, too," I said archly. "It had to be when my mom kept Danny and we had that candlelit dinner out overlooking the creek..."

"What can I say, I love making love to you under the sky?" he said.

"You can say you'll never stop," I said.

"I'll never stop, my love."

THE END

www.ingramcontent.com/pod-product-compliance
Lightning Source LLC
Chambersburg PA
CBHW030308160726
47992CB00005B/1929